# JULIET'S RULES
*(with additional notes by Sara)*

1. Drop something so he'll have to pick it up.
   *(Spaghetti in his lap is <u>not</u> a good idea)*

2. Order "what he's having."
   *(Unless you're allergic)*

3. Light candles.
   *(But <u>avoid</u> igniting the rest of his apartment)*

4. Wear enticing perfume.
   *(Unless HE'S allergic)*

5. Expect success....
   *(But maybe not with the man you expect...)*

Dear Reader,

Are there really rules for falling in love?

You see them on the bookstands, hear about them on talk shows and discuss them with your friends. Rules for falling in love, or maybe more important, rules for helping someone fall in love with you! But can following the rules really make love happen?

My answer? I don't know. But I will tell you that in the past few months, I've been blessed with finding a love of my own. Did I follow the rules? Some of them. Wouldn't you know that just like Sara and Matthew, and Dani and Alex, I've had the same doubts, fears and joys of opening my heart to another. And just like them, I've found some age-old wisdom to be a great source of comfort: Be honest. Love unconditionally. Take the risk.

So, dear reader, as you read these stories, I ask that you remember falling in love for the first time. Remember the advice that was given to you. And if you're so inclined, write to me and tell me about your rules for love. I'd love to share those moments and those memories with you.

Sincerely,

Jo Leigh

# HUSBAND 101

## JO LEIGH

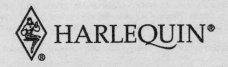

# HARLEQUIN®

TORONTO • NEW YORK • LONDON
AMSTERDAM • PARIS • SYDNEY • HAMBURG
STOCKHOLM • ATHENS • TOKYO • MILAN • MADRID
PRAGUE • WARSAW • BUDAPEST • AUCKLAND

This book is for Joe. You know why.

ISBN 0-373-16731-8

HUSBAND 101

## Juliet Renault's Thirty Steps To True Love

1. Drop something so he'll need to pick it up.
2. Make eye contact.
3. Touch his upper arm.
4. Practice witty conversations.
5. Mirror his movements.
6. Ask him a provocatively personal question. One he's never been asked before.
7. Play his favorite music.
8. Cook his favorite foods.
9. Give him a wicked smile.
10. Order "What he's having."
11. Laugh at his jokes.
12. Show him how loving you are to pets.
13. Make slow, seductive movements.
14. Make prolonged eye contact.
15. Smile!
16. Walk with self-confidence.
17. Wear his favorite color.
18. Get him to talk about himself.
19. Learn about his hobbies.
20. Light candles.
21. Compliment him.
22. Wear enticing perfume.
23. Loosen your body language.
24. Don't fidget.
25. Analyze his handwriting.
26. Get comfortable with condoms.
27. Expect success.
28. Be his friend.
29. Explore your femininity.
30. Cry fetchingly.

# *Chapter One*

Sara Cabot wondered what the Federal Express man would say if she asked, respectfully of course, to touch his behind. Or derriere as Juliet would say, her French accent making it sound like a Parisian dessert.

She sighed, knowing it didn't matter, because she would never have the courage to ask, respectfully or otherwise. Not her. It's not that she was a wimp in all things. Just about men. A lifetime of being with women, at home, at school, at the university, had left her with the skills necessary to do her job as a toy designer, run a household, keep her finances, even tune up her car, but absolutely no idea how to go about the business of dating.

She continued to eat her lettuce and tomato sandwich and stared longingly at the rear end of the delivery man. When he turned the corner, she put the sandwich down. She wasn't hungry anymore. Not for food anyway.

"You have that look about you, *chère amie.*"

Sara glanced up to see her friend and assistant, Juliet, standing at the door to their office. "I don't have any look," Sara said. "Except the usual."

Juliet shook her head as she walked over to her desk, directly across from Sara's. "I'd say Elliot was here, *non?*" She pointed to the packages on the floor by the back door. "I'm right. He was here, and you didn't talk to him, did you?"

Sara shook her head. Juliet was always encouraging her to speak to the men she met, and not about business. But Juliet was French, and she'd learned to flirt at two or something. Or maybe she didn't even have to learn. It was clearly hereditary, like her ivory complexion or her blue eyes. Even at sixty-five, Juliet received more appreciative glances than most of the women Sara knew, including herself.

"This is silly, Sara," Juliet said, her tone kind, but a little impatient. "You're twenty-six, lovely as a summer flower and lonely. When are you going to do something about it?"

Sara folded her paper lunch sack and tucked it under her purse. She tossed the uneaten half of her sandwich into the trash, and prepared to go back to work. "There isn't anything to do. I'm going to live and die a virgin, and they'll put my picture on the cover of the *Enquirer* when I'm gone."

"Haven't you learned anything from me?"

Sara smiled. "Men swoon for you, Juliet. Even

when they know you've been married thirty years. Me? They pat me on the head.''

"It's because you're shy, like a child. You have to take some chances. Risk. Being a virgin at your age, you should be ashamed.''

"I am. Believe me. I'm mortified. Maybe I'll hold a raffle. Give away a toaster to the first man who'll sleep with me.''

"You shouldn't joke like that. Giving yourself to a man is the most precious gift there is. It must be with someone extraordinary, who can see you for the remarkable girl you are.''

"I wish you'd find him for me, then. I'm not having any luck.''

Juliet stood, and walked over to the yellow guest chair near Sara's desk. She sat down, leaned forward and took Sara's hands in hers. "I've been thinking,'' she began.

"That makes me nervous.''

"Hush. *Écoutes.* I've been thinking that the only thing wrong with you is that you're untutored. You were too much with women. No father, no uncles. And that academy. For shame. Young girls and boys need to be together.''

"So, I need to go back to school? To a coed campus?''

Juliet shook her head, and a strand of silver hair came loose from her bun, gently curling all the way past her shoulder. No wonder she could still charm

Mr. Kelly. Twenty years her junior, and the vice president got all tongue-tied whenever he came near.

"Not school, *chérie*. Not a regular school, that is."

Sara's eyes narrowed even before she was fully cognizant of the fact that Juliet had A Plan. That wasn't a minor detail. Juliet's plans had gotten Sara into trouble far too often. "Hold it. Remember you told me to tell you when you were going off the deep end? Wasn't it just last month when you thought it would be wonderful to give the senior staff a little gift?"

"That was an exceptional cheese," Juliet said, straightening.

"It also smelled so bad after the long weekend they had to fumigate."

"Peasants. They don't realize richness always has strong presence."

"That kind of presence nearly got you fired. Not to mention what happened to Harriet."

Juliet lowered her eyes and shook her head. "Yes, Harriet. That was regrettable."

"So it's settled," Sara said, easing her hands from the older woman's grasp. "We'll leave well enough alone."

"But you're not well enough. And this is nothing like the cheese."

"Juliet," Sara said in her best Mother voice.

"Don't talk to me like that. Have respect for your elders."

Sara couldn't help but smile. "How come the only time you want respect is when you're cooking up some scheme? I swear, you're the French Lucy, and I don't want to be the American Ethel."

"Lucy got what she wanted most of the time, *non?*"

"What Lucy got was trouble."

"Adventure."

"Trouble."

"Excitement."

Sara's retort stuck in her throat. She'd made a tactical error and looked into Juliet's eyes. What she saw there was a world of daring, a leap in the dark, a life full of possibilities. Like a hypnotist's watch, Juliet's eyes chased away all the perfectly rational excuses Sara had lined up, until she was left with only a question. *What do I have to lose?* "What's the plan?" she asked, knowing she was going to regret it.

"I'm going to teach you."

"Teach me what?"

"Why, how to make love to a man, of course."

Sara's eyes widened. "I think there might be a slight translation problem here."

"Eh? You already know how to make a man fall to his knees? To want you more than he wants to breathe? To capture his heart and his soul?"

"No, I can't say that I do."

"Exactly. I will teach you."

"How?"

The smile on her friend's face was equal parts mischief and satisfaction. "I'm going to give you flirting lessons."

"We're not going to kiss, are we? I mean, I like you and all, but..."

"You're going to be kissed, *chérie,* but not by an old woman. You're going to finally know what it is to be loved by a man. A man who knows what he's doing."

"Not Elliot?" she said quickly.

Juliet swatted his name away. "That boy? Never. He has too many muscles up here," she said, pointing to her head. "He wouldn't know how to treat an orchid like you."

"Then who?"

Juliet paused. Her smile widened. "James Forester."

MATTHEW QUARTERMAIN heard laughter coming from Sara Cabot's office. Laughter from that area wasn't unusual. As a toy designer for Willard and Marsh, Ms. Cabot often had children in with her, and they did a lot of laughing. But this wasn't a child's giggle. The female voice rose above the din of the plant, even though the forklift was in action in the warehouse.

It was infectious, that laugh, and he would have smiled, if he'd been somewhere private.

He paused for a moment, trying to remember what he knew about Sara Cabot. Juliet Renault was her assistant. Sara was in her twenties, and from the sound, it was her laughing.

As he walked toward the docking bay the laughter grew dim, then disappeared, swallowed by the curses of the men off-loading the truck and the country music from someone's portable radio.

His gaze swept the area, checking for anything out of place. Nothing specific. Just something that would trip his own personal interior alarm system. The one that had made him a damn good Navy SEAL, and that would come in handy here at Willard and Marsh Toy Company.

It was that silent alarm, the click in his head, that had helped him discover the missing prototypes of the new Tiny Tina Teardrop doll. From there, it hadn't been difficult to trace other breaches of security. Now he knew someone was selling company secrets, someone from the inside. He wouldn't stop until he found that someone. It could be a janitor, a VP, or a purchasing agent. Because it could be anyone, he assumed it was everyone. No one got passed over. Every man and woman here was a suspect.

''Hey there, Mr. Quartermain.''

He stopped, looked to his right. An overly made-up assembler on the Portly Pig line had stopped work to wave at him. He scrambled for her name. He'd been here five weeks, and that was plenty of time to get to know the names of each of the hundred and four employees.

"Hello, Ms. Baskin."

"Honey, you can call me Terry."

"Thank you, Ms. Baskin, for the offer." He looked at his watch, then once again at her.

She got the point, turned immediately and picked up the plush pig she'd been working on. He did see her glance his way once more before he crossed over to the computer room.

Housing the main frame computer and all the CAD programs that were the heart of Willard and Marsh, the room was locked, chilly to protect the equipment and as sterile as possible.

At first, Matt had suspected that the thief worked in that rarefied area. The computer stored every one of the new toy prototype designs at each stage of manufacture. But endless hours of watching security tapes had led him nowhere.

He stood looking inside the glass walls, watching several men and two women work at separate keyboards. One of the women, Susan Gayle, caught him peeking and smiled.

She was a beautiful woman. He saw encouragement in her eyes. But he just nodded cordially, letting her know that he wasn't on the market.

He wasn't looking for a relationship, not even a casual affair. Not now. Not when he didn't know where he was going to be living, what his next job would be. And not after the fiasco that had been his one serious relationship. He'd need some time to get past that.

"You think it was one of them?"

He shrugged. He'd seen Ralph Marsh approach in the glass.

"Or someone else," he said. "It's too soon to tell."

"I heard from Larry English. He's working for Mattel now, and he heard that the Tiny Tina drawings were turning up in Japan."

"What company?" Matt turned to look at the president and CEO of Willard and Marsh.

"Unknown. He's checking."

"Let me talk to him," Matt said.

Ralph nodded. "I know you'll figure this out." He put his hand briefly on Matt's shoulder, then walked away toward the offices.

Matt watched him until he turned the corner, acutely aware of the confidence Marsh had in his abilities to catch the thief. Ralph had known his father, had served with his dad in the Navy. This job was an acknowledgment of that relationship, and more than anything, he wanted to do his father proud. He also wanted to save Ralph from this headache. Although it was never discussed, Matt knew that Ralph and his wife, Lilly, were having serious problems. Matt couldn't help on that score, but he could catch himself a thief.

His gaze went back to the clean room. To the glowing LED crystals and the lab-coated technicians. Someone was doing Ralph dirt, and that someone would pay.

SARA GIGGLED AGAIN, but cut it short. She'd lost it there for a minute. The very idea that she would get Jim Forester to fall in love with her was too absurd for words.

She'd upset Juliet, but honestly! This was her wildest scheme yet. Forester was not only the best-looking man in this company, maybe even the whole state, but he was also the most charming and desirable man she'd ever met. Not met, even. Heard about.

He was one of the chief topics of conversation among the female employees. When he worked out in the company gym, attendance soared. Tess Walker said she'd heard he was looking to get married. Terry Baskin had heard he'd been devastated by an ex-supermodel-girlfriend, and that he needed tender loving care to make him whole again. It was Denise Gillard who'd summed it up best, though. "I don't care who he's been with or how much he's hurt. That man can share my bed anytime he likes."

Leave it to Juliet to pick out a man like him for her cockeyed scheme. As if Forester would even look at her, let alone want her more than he wanted to breathe. The giggles were going to start again if she didn't watch it.

"Are you finished?" Juliet asked.

Sara nodded. Her friend had been quite peeved at her reaction. So peeved that she'd gone to her desk and worked for ten minutes without acknowledging that her office mate was in the throes of hysteria.

But Juliet's silent treatments never lasted long, and now she was studying Sara again, nodding at some secret decision. "We'll begin tomorrow."

"Juliet, my lovely friend, you can't be serious. It would be easier to go out with Mel Gibson than Jim Forester."

"Mel Gibson is married."

"That's not the point."

"I understand that you don't think you can do this. I do."

"But you're insane."

"Thank you very much."

Sara went over to Juliet's desk. "I meant that in the nicest way possible, of course."

"I want you to promise me," Juliet said, facing her with her earnest gaze.

"Promise what?"

"That you'll do what I ask."

"How can I promise that if I don't know what you've cooked up?"

"Because I care about you. You know I would never do anything to hurt you."

"Hurt? No. Embarrass? *Oui.*"

"*Chérie,* I don't mean to be harsh, but what has your method got you? Another Saturday night watching videos? Soup for one?"

"How humiliated am I going to be?"

"There can be no humiliation if you don't allow it."

Sara sighed. "That's easy for you to say. Nothing embarrasses you."

"That's right. Do you know why?"

"Because you're insane. I thought we'd already gone over that."

"Nonsense. It's because I don't care what others think. Who is so important, so special, to judge me? Or you? All these people with little lives, they walk in their sleep. They're so afraid that they miss all the joy, all the real pleasures. Don't be one of them, Sara. Don't let fear stop you from living your life."

Juliet's words sobered her up fast. Wasn't this exactly what she'd been praying for? A way to break out of her shell? To find the one thing she longed for with all her heart? "But Jim Forester?" she asked. "He's Mount Everest, and I'm not even ready for the bunny slope."

Juliet smiled. "But you see? That makes him perfect for our little experiment. If you can get Forester to notice you, to ask you out, to want you, then you can have any man you desire."

"So he's just the practice guy?"

"*Exactement.* The practice guy."

"And if he doesn't notice me?"

"If you do as I say, he'll notice you. I give you my word."

Sara knew she should go to her desk. Sit down, turn on her computer. Not even look in Juliet's direction. "This whole scheme has trouble written all over it," she said.

"Yes, Sara. And trouble is exactly what you need."

Closing her eyes, Sara thought about too many lonely nights. Her friends were wonderful, and she wouldn't trade them for the world, but they couldn't take the place of a man to love. Who would be in love with her. For that, she would give anything. Hadn't she whispered that a hundred nights, when sleep refused to come for the ache in her heart?

Sara nodded once. "All right," she said, even though she felt as if she was being shoved out of an airplane without a parachute. "I'll do it."

"Every step?"

She opened her eyes, and met Juliet's gaze. "Every step."

THE NEXT MORNING, while Sara was still working on her first cup of coffee, Juliet gave her the notebook. It was spiral bound with a red cover, like something she'd taken to school. It looked innocent enough. But when she opened it and got a look at what was written, she nearly passed out.

"Touch his arm? Mirror his movements? Wear his favorite color? Cook his favorite foods? Are you kidding?"

"Uh-uh. Remember your promise."

"But—"

"No buts. All you have to do is follow step by step. Look how easy the first one is."

"Drop something?"

"Yes. A handkerchief."

"I don't own one."

"Then use your imagination. Today, you go to the cafeteria. He's there on Wednesdays, *non?* Drop your fork. He'll pick it up and hand it to you."

"Not if I drop it in the ladies room," she muttered.

"That's no way to begin," Juliet said. "Think of this as a great adventure. A challenge."

"It's a challenge, all right. I just don't know if I'm capable."

"Of course you are. You're strong, stronger than you know."

"Will you come with me?"

Juliet shook her head. "No, *chérie.* This is a journey you must make alone."

"Will you pay for my funeral when I die of embarrassment?"

"Put that thought away. It has no place. Courage, Sara. I know you can do this."

Sara continued reading the handwritten notes, growing more dismayed with each step. Thirty in all. All the way from smiling at his jokes, to learning about his hobbies. She shook herself, reminded herself of nights alone with Lean Cuisine. Even climbing Mount Everest started with the first step. How hard could it be? She'd dropped her fork plenty of times. But still…order what he's having?

"You know this could set the women's movement back fifty years."

"Would you rather be politically correct, or happy?"

She shut the book and took in a deep breath. "All right," she said. "I promised, and I'll go through with it."

"Wonderful."

"So tell me, how will I know when I've passed Flirting 101?"

"You'll know, *chérie*. Believe me. You'll know."

## Chapter Two

Matt studied the array of foods in the cafeteria with indifference. Nothing appealed, not even the spaghetti. Until recently, he had enjoyed food. He'd even cooked a bit. Well, omelettes and spaghetti, but they were great omelettes and fantastic spaghetti. Now, one thing was as good as another, so he grabbed a big salad and a piece of fish.

His appetite wasn't the only thing that had changed since the accident. His morning workout had become a chore, where it used to be a challenge. He had to remind himself to pick up between weekly maid visits, where he used to be a stickler for neatness. He was having trouble finishing books. He'd find them open in the bedroom or in the living room, and have no desire to start them again. Even Tom Clancy.

His attention seemed to be focused in only one direction—finding out who was stealing from Willard and Marsh. When he tried to think about his future, whether he was going to stay on here or move to Washington, he'd get distracted. It had happened so many times that he was certain it was psychologically-based. Avoidance. What he didn't know was why.

He spotted Jim's table in the center of the room. The same table they'd shared last Wednesday and the Wednesday before. On his way he noted the quick and easy conversations of long-time employees. Several women smiled in his direction, but his response was merely polite. Even women had become something to put up with, like the traffic and the news. He just couldn't seem to get excited about anyone. Which, ironically, didn't seem to have any effect on his libido. He wanted a woman that way, he just didn't want to get involved.

He put his food on the table and stacked his tray, then sat across from Jim. He was grateful for the man's company, mostly because he required very little in the conversation department.

As he put his napkin on his lap, he cased the area, noting the regulars, the occasionals, the ones he didn't recognize. There were two men, both in dark suits, sitting with Kelly, the VP of operations. He'd have to check that out.

Sandy from payroll smiled at him, and he briefly wondered if she meant to signal him or his table partner. Jim attracted more than his fair share of attention from the ladies, and even Matt could see why. He was a good-looking man, and he knew how to use it.

Sandy smiled once more, and this time he knew it was for him. She was attractive, and from what he'd heard, bright and funny. But, like the spaghetti, it just wasn't important enough to act on.

He ate. The fish was bland and so was the salad. It didn't matter.

He watched. The employees were animated or serious, chatty or quiet. It didn't matter.

His internal signals hadn't been triggered. No one was up to no good, or if they were, they were keeping it hidden.

Halfway through the meal, however, something shifted. His head came up, his back straightened. He was on full alert status, and his gaze swept the room with laser intensity, then stopped when he got to the woman standing by the cashier.

He knew her. No, he'd seen her. Sara Cabot. The laughing woman from yesterday. Ideas were her game, and she was at the top of her form. If anyone knew what cutting-edge toy technology was worth, it would be Sara Cabot. A very nervous Sara Cabot.

It was her anxiousness that had alerted him. Her jerky movements, seen peripherally, but seen. The very air around her was charged with tension.

He watched her pay for her meal and noticed her hand quiver. Taking the opportunity, he cataloged her features, her manner of dress, the way she fidgeted.

She was pretty. That much he'd remembered from before. She was slim, maybe slightly underweight, but instead of looking skinny, she seemed delicate. Her hair was long, deep brown, pushed back with a thin band. She dressed modestly, a simple skirt and blouse, plain pumps. But something didn't add up. She was as tense as a high wire, yet now that she was walking toward him, he could see her innate grace. She walked with her toes pointed out slightly, like a ballerina.

She reminded him of someone. He kept watching her approach. Fearful, elegant. Audrey Hepburn. That was it. She looked like a young Hepburn, with that long neck and those doe eyes. That same fragility.

Could she be stealing company secrets? A pretty thing like her? Unfortunately he knew the answer to that was yes. Looks had nothing to do with what was in a person's heart.

It occurred to him that while he was watching her so studiously, she was also watching him. She knew he was security, so she'd be wise to keep him in sight, but she was staring, openly, and heading right toward him. That didn't make sense. Or maybe it did.

She focused on Jim now, not him. She had that same look about her, though. She didn't stop biting her lower lip, and her steps got even more hesitant. A few seconds later, she'd turned once more to look in Matt's direction.

He met her gaze, and she froze for a second, a pink tinge coloring her cheeks. She didn't blink for a long while, as if what she saw terrified her. Then she swallowed, he could see that from here, and continued walking.

When she reached his side, he expected her to say something. He even looked up, waiting.

Instead she smiled apprehensively at Jim, then tipped her tray and poured her entire plate of spaghetti and sauce directly on Matt's lap.

SARA STARED DOWN at Matthew Quartermain's crotch. The spaghetti and sauce had made a direct hit, squarely on his upper, *upper* thighs. Some had hit the floor, but only a few drops. Mostly it had hit the bull's-eye.

She looked back at her tray. The stupid fork was still there. Then she looked back at what she had dropped. All she could think of was a single desire—for the earth to open and swallow her whole.

She glanced at Jim Forester, but his grin made her flinch. Matthew stood slowly, taking his own plate and transferring some of the mess to that. The stain was hideous and large. She could only imagine how it felt, and prayed it wasn't too hot.

Matt Quartermain was the last person on earth she wanted to douse with spaghetti. He was without question the scariest man she'd ever met. His demeanor was always serious, his eyes observant and quick. She'd heard he was an ex-Navy SEAL, and looking at his muscular frame, she believed it.

They'd never spoken, and she'd been fine with that. And now she'd gone and done this!

She expected him to do something, to get furious, to yell. She didn't want to meet his eye, but she couldn't make her feet run. Finally, she did look up.

He wasn't just dumbfounded. He was downright flabbergasted. She felt her face heat with the mother of all blushes, her heart pound like a tom-tom in her chest. She'd tried one simple thing. Number one on the list. Now she'd not only flubbed things with her "practice guy" but she'd covered the head of security with tomato sauce and pasta and they both clearly thought—no, *knew*—she was completely nuts.

Quartermain squinted at her, then became alarmed. "Are you okay?" he said.

"Me?"

He nodded. "You look a little…"

"I— It was supposed to be the fork."

"The fork?"

She nodded. "Did I burn you?"

He shook his head. "Surprised the hell out of me, though."

The shock that had held her still left abruptly, replaced immediately with a crystalline and precise awareness that she had made a colossal ass of herself in front of most of the company, and that she was still batting a thousand by standing there like a dope.

She put her tray down and grabbed the napkins.

She attacked the problem head-on, wiping his pants furiously. "I'm so sorry," she said, her words as quick as her hand. "I didn't mean to—I never would have—"

He reached down and grasped her wrist, holding it still. She was bent forward, and so intent on fixing her mistake that she'd barely noticed the area she was so studiously cleaning.

"I think I can take care of that, Ms. Cabot. But thanks for your efforts."

If there was a gold medal for humiliation, Sara had a lock on it. She withdrew her hand from his crotch, trying desperately not to look. But because she realized she shouldn't look, that looking would make things infinitely worse, that a person with any manners whatsoever would never look, her gaze went to his zipper and stayed there.

And because the universe had a wicked sense of humor, something moved. Right there. Just behind the zipper. Under all that spaghetti sauce. It didn't move much. But, and this she would remember distinctly in the months ahead, it did, in fact, move.

Finally, with the help of a tardy guardian angel, she stood up, shifting her gaze to his face.

Now he was blushing. It was subtle, not like her glowing neon. Just a nice, discreet shade of pink, high on his cheeks.

"All through?" he asked.

The irony was not lost on her. She nodded, and did her best to smile. "I'll pay for the cleaning bill."

"That won't be necessary."

"I feel just awful."

"No need. Mistakes happen."

"Please don't be so nice about this. It makes it worse."

"Well, I suppose I could shout if it would make you feel better."

Sara shook her head. "No, no. That wouldn't help, either."

"Would you like to go lie down or something? There's a couch in my office."

"No! I mean, thank you, but no. I'm fine. Just embarrassed."

"I'm sure no one noticed a thing."

She looked around for the first time since she'd tipped her tray. Everyone was staring. Bill Williams was standing on his chair. Several people were wiping tears from their eyes. "Right," she said. "No one noticed."

He looked around, too, and she saw his jaw tighten. He took her arm and said, "Let's go."

She looked back at Jim Forester, the man she was supposed to charm and entice. He seemed deeply amused, and she knew he was not laughing with her, but at her. Great beginning.

Matt escorted her through the cafeteria, looking straight ahead, not acknowledging the stares or the pointing. There was a dignity in his gait that she envied, but couldn't emulate. She wondered how hard it was going to be to find another job. In Alaska.

Once they were out of the cafeteria, but not out of earshot, the room erupted with laughter. That was the last straw. She pulled herself free from his grip, and without so much as a goodbye, she ran away.

Matt watched her round the corner. She was making pretty good time. He just hoped she wouldn't run into the tray carts that were—

The resounding crash of breaking glass, of metal on metal, made him wince.

He walked toward the men's room, shaking his head, wondering what the hell had just happened. That was no accident. He'd seen her deliberately tip her tray. She must have known that the spaghetti would land on his lap, but then she'd gotten that look of surprise that seemed completely genuine.

He pushed open the bathroom door, grateful to see he was alone. As he wiped his pants, he remembered the feel of her busy hands and his completely involuntary reaction. Then the look on her face.

His smile turned into laughter and for a moment he just let go. When he was through, he settled down, sighed and got back to business. He'd have to go home and change, but he tried to do the best he could anyway. Besides, he needed an uncluttered moment to look at this thing rationally.

One, Sara had looked as nervous as a rookie on her first dive. Two, her nervousness had something to do with him. Three, she'd intentionally poured her lunch on his lap. Four, she had access to the computerized plans for the Tiny Tina doll and had ample opportunity to do a little dealing on the side. Five, she'd made him laugh. For the first time in a long, long time.

He smiled again, just thinking of her staring at his zipper, and it felt odd, but good. He'd grown unaccustomed to smiling, to laughing. To feeling much of anything.

Sara Cabot had certainly gotten his attention. Now, all he had to do was make sure that she wasn't stealing the company blind.

"IT WAS THE MOST HORRIBLE moment of my life," she said. "Beyond humiliation. There isn't a word for how awful it was. I quit."

"No, no, no," Juliet said as she locked the office door. "You did just what you were supposed to."

Sara looked at her unbelievingly. "I poured hot food on Matt Quartermain's lap!"

"You got Jim's attention, no?"

"I'll say. And everyone else's attention, too. I'm a laughingstock."

"Half the women in this company are kicking themselves that they didn't do it first."

"What planet are you from? This was not a good thing. This was bad. Very, very bad."

Juliet went to the desk and perched on the edge, right near where Sara's head was cradled in her hands. "You're looking at this all wrong, *chérie*. You're only thinking in the short-term. In the long run, what you did was perfect. It got his attention, it gave you both an amusing story to tell, and if you let it, it will give you confidence."

"Confidence?"

"Of course."

Sara thought of looking around for a hidden camera. "I must not have explained this well," she said. "I can't show my face around here any more. I have to quit, move out of the state. Maybe even the country."

Juliet laughed, but not unkindly. "This is why you must continue with all the steps in our little book."

"Oh, no. Not a chance."

"Yes, it's important for you to learn the perspective of a seasoned adult. Not the slim view of a child."

"I don't think this is a matter of perspective. Bill Williams stood on his chair to see better."

"Then he is a child, too."

"You are too much for me, Juliet. Maybe in France this would be a little amusing story. Here, it's a candidate for 'America's Funniest Home Videos.'"

"What did he say to you?"

"When?"

"After you spilled your plate."

She thought for a minute, remembering certain

details, like the way Matthew's pants sort of grew, but struggling with others. "Jim didn't say a word. He was too busy laughing. It was Quartermain who talked to me. He asked if I was all right."

"Hmm."

"I don't like the sound of that."

"Matthew Quartermain you say? I hadn't considered him."

"Considered him for what?"

Juliet stared at her for a moment, but her concentration was somewhere else. Planning more humiliating exercises no doubt.

"Juliet? Why are you smiling like that?"

"Smiling like what? I'm pleased for you, Sara. You were perfect."

"Perfect?"

"James saw you, dear. He paid attention, not to the silly circumstance, but to you. This is very good."

"If you think I'm going to continue with this stupid little game—"

Juliet stood up, grabbing Sara's attention. Her face had lost its sympathetic mien. "Sara Cabot, do you want to live the rest of your life as a little caterpillar at the edge of the cornfield? As a little mouse hiding in the cupboard? Or do you want to be someone of substance. Someone whose life matters?"

She swallowed. "I didn't mean to make you angry," she said.

"I'm not angry. I'm frustrated. You've got so much, *chérie,* so much to give. I know that heart of yours is bigger than the moon, and yet you sit at your small flat and let it grow fallow. You have an opportunity to change everything. To feel what it's like to truly live. If you let a little embarrassment stop you now, you may never get this chance again."

"You seriously expect me to go on? To continue?"

"Of course. The ball is already rolling."

She shook her head. "No. The next time he sees me, he's going to run for the hills. He thinks I'm a nutcase, or at least incredibly clumsy."

"He probably doesn't know what to think of you. But I'll wager he wants to find out."

"I'm sorry to disappoint you, Juliet. I know you want what's best for me, but I can't do it."

"It's not me you're disappointing, Sara."

She met her friend's gaze, and smiled sadly. "You're probably right. But I'm not brave like you."

"I see." Juliet went back to her desk. She turned to her computer and began to work.

Sara didn't like that she'd lost Juliet's respect. She was a good friend, one of her closest. And Sara admired her as much as anyone in her life. But she just couldn't go on. Not after the way she'd bungled—

Her phone interrupted, and she picked up the receiver.

"Sara Cabot."

"Ms. Cabot?"

It wasn't him. It was worse. It was Matthew Quartermain. She slammed the phone down.

"That was Quartermain, wasn't it?" Juliet said.

Sara blinked. "How did you know?

"Just a hunch."

"What does he want?"

"I don't know. But it would probably work better if you didn't hang up on him next time."

She'd hung up on him. Slammed the phone down. She lowered her head to her hands. "Oh, just shoot me now."

The phone rang.

Sara let it ring three, four times. Then she lifted it tentatively to her ear. "Sara Cabot."

"Don't hang up."

It was him. The dark man with the light blue eyes. The man the others talked about in a whisper. Suddenly she couldn't breathe.

"Hello?"

"Yes," she said, her voice high with uncontrolled nerves.

"I wanted to make sure you were all right. You looked a little shaky back there."

She blinked several times. Looked at Juliet's smug grin. Wondered if this was a secret plot to get even. "I'm—"

"Hello?"

"Okay," she said, wondering when she'd relinquished her body to the alien inside her.

"That's good," he said, and she could hear the grin in his voice.

"How are you? Are you burned?"

"No. Just a little stained."

"I didn't mean to touch your—" She froze.

"You were very thoughtful," he said. "But enough about that. Are you planning to go to the cocktail party tomorrow night?"

She nodded.

"Hello?"

"Yes," she said.

"Good. I'll see you then."

"Okay."

"Will you do me a favor?"

"Okay."

"Stick to cold hors d'oeuvres."

He hung up, and she listened to nothing for a while. Then she figured out how to move her hand, and she replaced the receiver.

"He's going to see me at the cocktail party tomorrow night," she said, not knowing what to think.

"I'm glad," Juliet said.

Sara looked at her. "Why? He's the wrong man."

"Maybe."

"What does that mean?"

"Nothing. Jim Forester will also be at the party."

"It doesn't matter. I'm not going."

Juliet shook her head. "You're going. And Mr. Forester won't be able to take his eyes off you."

"But I did everything wrong."

"No, Sara. You did everything just right. Now, relax. You've gotten your embarrassment over with. The rest will run like clockwork."

# Chapter Three

Matt looked up from the employee file as Jim walked into his office.

"What's up?" Jim asked, making himself comfortable in the leather chair across from Matt's desk.

"What do you know about Sara Cabot?"

Jim's grin was quick. "She has good aim."

"Funny," he said, not meaning it. "What do you really know?"

Jim reached up and loosened his tie. "Not much. She's quiet. Great with the focus groups. She's known for her dolls. Let's see, there was the Paisley Princess, Emily, Cry Baby and, of course, Tiny Tina."

"And personally?"

Jim shook his head. "I don't have a clue. I've never seen her outside of work." His gaze narrowed. "Why? You think she might have something to do with the stolen prototypes?"

Matt nodded. "There's something suspicious

about Sara Cabot, that much I know. She was always such a little mousy thing, until now.''

"You think she's the thief?''

"I don't know. But she is a suspect. So I want you to keep an eye on her.''

"That's not going to be hard. I couldn't help but notice she was damned attractive, even with that royal blush.''

"Attractive or not, I want to make sure she's clean. Talk to her. Get her to like you.''

Jim's smile turned rakish. "It's a tough job, but someone's got to do it.''

"Never mind. I'll do it myself.''

"No, no. I can handle it, boss.''

Matt shifted in his chair. This wasn't going the way he'd planned. It had been a mistake, calling Jim in here. He liked Forester. The guy was good at his job, and he'd become a friend. But Matt didn't care for the salacious way he spoke about Sara. Which made no sense empirically, but set off alarm bells nonetheless. There was something inherently innocent about her. The way she'd blushed, the way she'd wiped his pants. Her actions seemed genuine. Except...

He couldn't stop thinking about her. There could be only one explanation for that. He'd picked up some subtle clue that she was not what she seemed. Something was suspicious about Sara Cabot, and he was going to find out what that something was.

"Are we done? I've got some work to do.''

Matt stood up and walked Jim to the door. "Thanks for coming by," he said. "No need to go overboard with this. Just pay attention to her. Let her get comfortable with you. Let me know if something seems fishy."

"It's my honor to serve," Jim said. "And my pleasure."

Matt smiled, but when Jim left the grin faded quickly. He didn't like the tight sensation in his gut, or the way he couldn't get her out of his thoughts.

He'd been played for a fool by a woman too much like Sara Cabot. He wouldn't let that happen again.

SARA WAS HOLDING COURT, and doing a damn fine job of it. Matt sat near the door, trying to be as unobtrusive as possible in this creative meeting. Jim was sitting at the head of the large conference table, and Ralph was at the other end. In between sat the whole team. Juliet Renault took notes. Bill Williams chewed absently on his thumbnail. Kerry Wise doodled on his notepad. And Paulie Rose sipped her tea. But they all listened.

Sara talked about the new Tiny Tina doll. She'd done her homework and it showed. Matt had a hard time reconciling the woman in this meeting, this businesslike, calm professional with the woman who'd dumped her spaghetti in his lap.

She had control of the room, and she knew it. By the time she got to the part where she asked for additional funds, there was no question she would get them. Her arguments had been so well laid out, he figured she'd make a decent Navy SEAL. She'd be cool under fire, and she'd motivate her men to go farther, dig deeper, fly higher. She even got Williams to stop gnawing on his finger.

The only thing that spoiled the picture was her reaction to him. She'd blushed wildly when he walked into the meeting. After that, she'd avoided looking in his direction. Completely. She wouldn't meet his gaze.

Guilt? Or just embarrassment over yesterday's food toss? He had to lean toward the former. Sara was too sure of herself to be undone by a plate of spaghetti. Guilt also made sense after he'd found out about her financial situation.

She supported her mother and grandmother, and although she had a very nice salary, it wouldn't allow for any luxuries. Money was tight, and some lucre from the competition would go a long way. She drove a seven-year-old car. She rented a one-bedroom duplex, and paid the mortgage on her mother's house. Yet, watching her, feeling her enthusiasm for her job, her passion for her product, he had to wonder yet again.

Maybe she wasn't selling secrets voluntarily. Blackmail might be involved. Or not. Whatever the truth was, he needed to find out quickly. She upset his life too much. Made him think about things better left alone. Like what it would be like to touch that hair of hers. Or kiss that neck.

He stood up abruptly. Every eye turned toward him, and he got the feeling that Sara had stopped talking in the middle of a sentence.

He cleared his throat. "Excuse me," he said, then quickly went for the door. Once he was outside he took a deep breath. What the hell? He had no business thinking about Sara Cabot's hair or her neck. He had no business getting hot, no business feeling flushed.

Of all the women in this company, or even in this city, Sara was the one person he shouldn't be thinking about that way. He didn't know all about her, but he did know that she was naive. Young, untried, she'd barely been out in the world long enough to learn anything. Especially about sex.

She'd gone to girls' schools. She had no brothers. She'd even attended a women's college, for heaven's sake. She was a babe in the woods, and as far as he was concerned that meant she was strictly taboo.

"ANY QUESTIONS?"

Jim leaned forward. "What's the top of the age group we're shooting for here?"

Sara didn't have to look at her notes. "Ten at the outside. But the bulk of our audience is going to be six through eight. That's why we need to make Tina as sturdy as we can. She'll be thrown around quite a bit, and we don't want her to stop wetting after a month or two."

"So you think they'll want to buy diapers separately?"

"I'd rather they didn't have to. We could include a spare in the packaging."

Sara listened as Jim picked up the ball and ran with it. He was going for economy, which was his job, but she knew she'd made her points well. Despite the presence of the security man.

Once Matt Quartermain walked into the room, it was all she could do not to run back to her office. It had gotten worse as the minutes ticked by, and his gaze never wavered from her face. She was incredibly grateful that she'd been so prepared for this meeting.

The odd thing was her reaction to Jim Forester. He'd smiled at her, and she'd smiled back. Nothing. No blush. No tense tummy. Just smiles.

Then Matt had come into the room, and she'd fallen apart. Was it all due to the spaghetti incident? Yes, of course. What else could it be?

"Congratulations, Sara."

She looked up to see Jim standing by her chair. She'd zoned there for a moment, and now the meeting was at an end. "Thank you," she said, figuring she'd gotten her budget raised. Why else would he be congratulating her?

"You coming to the party tonight?"

She stood up. "Yes, of course," she said, making her decision that moment. "It's my project. I wouldn't miss it for the world."

"Good," he said, his gaze intent. "I'll see you there."

Sara's hand went to her throat. "Great."

Jim nodded, then turned to leave.

"You see?" Juliet whispered from behind her. "It's already working."

Sara waited until Jim was outside to turn to her friend.

"Nothing's working," she said softly. "He's just being polite."

"He's already under your spell."

Sara sighed. "You should really be a writer, Juliet. You have such a wonderful imagination."

"Thank you. Now get your things. You have to leave in ten minutes."

"Why?"

"I've made an appointment for you at the Golden Door. You're going to get a makeover."

Sara took a step back. "Oh, no. My makeup is just fine, thank you. I don't need it made over."

"Remember your promise?"

Bill Williams stepped past Sara and gave her a broad smile. "You did good, kiddo," he said.

"Thank you."

"Do me a favor?"

She smiled expectantly.

"Next time, drop your spaghetti on Jim, will ya? He needs it a lot more than Quartermain."

Sara blushed once more. Shouldn't there be a

limit on blushes? If you go crimson five times in one day, you become immune?

Bill laughed on his way out, and she looked to make sure she and Juliet were truly alone. "I can't do this."

"Of course you can. And you will. You're going to be gorgeous tonight, *chérie. Très jolie.*"

"Why do I get the feeling that's what the wolf said to Little Red Riding Hood before he ate her?"

"I'm not the wolf you have to beguile."

"Well you're no innocent granny, either."

Juliet smiled wickedly. "Thank goodness."

SARA STOOD OUTSIDE the restaurant, hesitant to walk in. She could get her car back from the valet and no one would be the wiser. She'd tell them she'd come down with a headache. No one would suspect a thing.

This cocktail party wasn't mandatory. Although, since it was celebrating the launch of Tiny Tina, her baby, it would look mighty peculiar if she weren't there. Especially with all the trouble over the prototypes.

Okay, so she had to go in. Maybe she could head straight to the bathroom and pull off the false eyelashes. That shouldn't be too hard. Everyone has to go to the rest room.

She squared her shoulders, feeling very much like one of her painted dolls, and walked inside.

The room was abuzz with conversation. Willard

and Marsh had rented the restaurant for the evening, so she recognized almost everyone there. She didn't see Juliet, or Jim. But she did see Matt.

He'd turned her way the moment she walked in the door. He'd been about to take a drink, but he'd stopped just short. It was a moment she'd remember for a long while. A mixture of embarrassment, recognition, awareness. Just like in the movies, everyone around him dimmed into a fuzzy blur. The light from above hit him like a spotlight. She noted his hair, and how the dark strands seemed to be a little damp. His suit. Nothing as fancy or tailored as Jim's usual attire, but sharp and well-fitting, elegantly simple. His face. Stern, with his square jaw, thick brows and those startling blue eyes.

Her chest tightened, and for the first time she fully understood it had nothing to do with spilling her food on his lap. This was something different. Something she didn't understand.

"Champagne?"

The voice to her left made her jump, which scared the young waiter. He almost lost the tray of neatly filled flutes, but he saved it with an impressive lunge.

"I'm sorry," she said. "I didn't know you were there."

The waiter smiled graciously. "No problem. Would you like a drink?"

She shook her head. "The rest room?"

He pointed with his free hand. She'd have to walk

by Matt in order to get there. She felt that chest tightness again. Why did he intimidate her so? Was it his job? His muscular body? The way he seemed to look through her?

Ridiculous. She smiled at the nice waiter and went for it. She nodded at all the friendly hellos, made promises to return in one second. She even felt a little secret pleasure at the many compliments that came her way.

Maybe the makeover hadn't been such a mistake. More than one of her male co-workers said, "Wow," which was a compliment she could really understand. "Wow," was before planning, it was the mouth reacting before the head got in the act. "Wow," was downright wonderful.

"You look fantastic."

She stopped so suddenly she almost caused another accident. But the voice to her right was unmistakable. Her target. Jim Forester.

"I mean it. You look great."

She turned, trying to remember tonight's lesson plan. One, to touch him meaningfully on the arm. That shouldn't be hard. Two, on the other hand, was a little trickier. Primp to show off her femininity. She'd balked and whined about that one, but Juliet had been adamant.

"This man only sees you in a work environment," she'd said. "Now you can show him there's a woman inside."

Sara decided to work on number one, and deal with "two" later. "Hi."

Jim smiled in a way that should have pleased her. It was warm, inviting, somewhat sinful. Instead she felt foolish again. As if she were in a very bad play.

"You haven't been to the bar yet?" he asked.

She shook her head. He signaled the waiter, then faced her again. "Champagne first, for the toast, okay?"

She nodded. If this kept up, she may not have to speak at all.

"You've been keeping secrets," he said.

"What do you mean?"

"You've been hiding that body of yours behind all those long skirts and buttoned blouses."

She looked down at the dress Juliet had picked out for her. It was simple, black. And formfitting. Not her style at all. "Oh, this," she said. "It's not really me."

"I'd say it was you twice over," he said. "Brains and beauty. That's some combination."

"Thank you," she said, anxious to drop the subject. She'd never mastered the art of accepting personal compliments, although Juliet had insisted that the only necessary response was a thank-you. It felt awkward, though. Just as awkward as standing next to Jim Forester, waiting to make her move.

Touch him meaningfully. Hand to arm. Upper arm. Maintain eye contact.

First she had to get eye contact. She moved a bit

to her left so that the light would hit her in the face. Then she stared at him. He didn't stare back. First his gaze moved around the room, presumably looking for the drinks. Then he looked at her chest, presumably looking for her breasts. He looked there for a long time.

She wasn't Sophia Loren, but by God she wasn't a boy. He should have found what he was searching for by now. She cleared her throat.

He dragged his gaze upward until he reached her eyes. "So tell me about yourself, Sara Cabot. What makes you tick?"

She almost answered, then remembered step eighteen. "I'm much more interested in hearing about you."

His posture changed, and his smile reached his eyes. She had to give credit where it was due. Juliet certainly knew about men. It was clear his question about her background had been perfunctory, and that he'd much rather talk about himself.

"What can I say," Jim said, "I'm just a working man with a typical dream. Wife, kids, white picket fence. And a nice fat savings account in the Cayman Islands." He laughed, and she did, too, wondering which part of his confession was a joke.

But perhaps she wasn't being fair. She'd never heard any negative gossip about Jim, well, except for his proclivity to play musical beds. But that was a rumor, not a fact. Most importantly, Juliet had recommended Jim for this little project, and Juliet was the most intuitive woman she'd ever met.

"What brought you to toys?" she asked, struggling to maintain eye contact, which was difficult, since Jim clearly wanted to see everything going on around him more than he wanted to look at her.

"I could tell you it was because of my love for children. But you wouldn't buy that, would you?"

She shook her head absently. She'd given up on the eye contact and was now in maneuvering position to attempt the arm touch.

"The truth is, I was recruited here just after college. Originally I was in sales, but I worked my way up the ladder."

She had to make her move now. Touch his upper arm. Not shoulder. Casually, as if she did this every day. But just as she moved forward, he moved back, and she lunged, panicking at the sudden shift.

She saw the waiter a split second before she hit him. The crash itself was almost poetic. The look of surprise on the young man's face was the very essence of drama. The arc of the tray combined with the spray of champagne deserved slow-motion photography and a rousing musical score. The sound of the individual flutes smashing on the tile floor seemed almost majestic. Then there was the collective gasp from the audience. And, of course, the laughter.

Sara was unable to move. She was rooted to the spot, transfixed by what she had wrought. Terrified that if she took even one step another great calamity would fall on her head. An earthquake maybe. Or an avalanche.

Someone touched her arm. Gently. The upper part of her arm. Just like from her book. She turned, and saw it was Matthew Quartermain.

"You okay?" he asked.

She nodded then looked at his hand, still touching her arm. "That's what it was supposed to be like."

"Huh?"

"You know. Your hand. Like the fork."

"Uh-huh," he said slowly. "Why don't you come with me. We'll find someplace you can sit down."

"No. I'd better not. I'll just stand right here until everyone goes home. It's for the best." When she looked up at him, he was smiling. Much, much nicer than Jim Forester's smile. This one changed his face, made him seem friendly, not at all daunting. "You should do that more often," she said.

"What?"

"Smile."

He looked down with an endearing humility, then back at her. "I guess I'll just have to stick close to you."

"That could be life-threatening."

"Come on, Sara. Let's let our friend here clean up."

She saw now that the poor waiter was picking up

the broken glass, piling the remains on the wet silver tray. "I'll help," she said.

"No!"

She looked around. The cry hadn't just come from the waiter, but from Jim, Bill, Stephanie, Laura and Juliet. A whole chorus telling her to stay away. Great. Now everyone thought she was dangerous. Or crazy. Or both.

"Very funny," Matt said, slightly tightening his hold on her arm. She let him lead her away from the mess, all the way to the back of the restaurant. He watched her slide into the booth. "Stay put," he said.

Naturally, she didn't argue. While he was gone, she had plenty of time to relive her latest humiliation, and more than enough time to use every curse she'd ever heard. She even made one up. The game was over, no matter what Juliet said. She couldn't take any more of this.

Matt's shadow fell on the table, and she carefully turned to him using only her head. She didn't dare try anything more. He held two glasses.

"I hope you like bourbon," he said.

She nodded. "I hope it's a triple."

He put her glass down, then scooted into the booth across from her. "Nope, just a nice bourbon and Seven. It'll calm you down a bit."

"Calm? I don't need calm. I need euthanasia."

"Now, it's not that bad."

"No?"

"It's nothing a little spit and polish won't take care of. Hell, you livened up what has got to be one of the dullest parties on record. You did fine."

"Did Juliet send you here?"

His bewildered look told her more than his "No."

"Okay, then." She sipped her drink and welcomed the soft burn that traveled down her throat. Drinking was not one of her favorite things, but tonight it seemed a wise and prudent thing to do.

"You were good today," Matt said quietly. "In the meeting, I mean."

Sara studied his face, but she didn't detect sarcasm. "Thank you. Why were you there? I've never seen you at one of them before."

"I was there because of you."

"Me?"

He nodded, then took a healthy swig of his drink. "I wanted to see you in action."

"Why? Because of the spaghetti?"

"Partly."

"You know, before all this happened, I was a perfectly normal person. I didn't drop food on people or crash into waiters."

"Before all this?"

She'd said too much. There was no way she was going to admit to her flirting lessons. Not to him, or any man. But especially not him. "Before I met you." She was grateful for the save. It wasn't a lie, either.

"I'm flattered."

"Huh? Oh, my," she mumbled, staring at her drink. She didn't know how to respond to that. She couldn't tell if he was just being nice because she'd made such a fool of herself, or if he was making an honest friendly gesture.

Any schoolgirl would have been able to interpret his signals, she thought. Any normal twenty-six-year-old woman wouldn't have had to try. Yet she was clueless. She couldn't even look at him. Should she smile? Act aloof? Run? He wasn't even her practice man, and she was completely out of her league. How would she ever get Jim to fall in love with her when she couldn't even speak to Matt Quartermain? Suddenly a life of celibacy wasn't looking so bad. She'd get cats. Lots and lots of cats.

"What are you two cooking up back here?"

Sara looked up at the sound of Jim's voice. He smiled down at her with humor, although as she let her gaze travel she saw spots of champagne all over his suit. Champagne didn't stain, at least. Not like spaghetti sauce.

She took another swallow of her drink. A big one.

"We're just talking," Matt said. "Nothing special."

"So scoot over," Jim said, motioning toward her. "I can talk about nothing special better than anyone."

Matt smiled, but it wasn't quite as warm as she would have imagined. She knew the two men were friends. Jim was practically the only person in the company Matt talked with. So why the tension between them?

As she faced both of her recent victims, one to her left and one straight ahead, she quickly reviewed the opportunities for disaster that lay at hand. She could spill her drink. She could say something stupid. She could blush until her face burst like a balloon. There was even a reasonable chance that she could throw up. Now *that's* flirting.

"Why the smile?" Jim asked.

She shook her head, carefully. "Nothing. Just trying to enjoy what's left of the party."

He smiled back at her, anchored her gaze, then touched her upper arm with a brief, yet meaningful squeeze. Juliet would love him, she thought. He'd mastered steps two and three without a falter.

"You're the only bright spot at this shindig," he said, keeping his gaze steady. "You got Mrs. Klemper in the face, you know. With her own drink. She just yelped, then tossed her champagne right in her own kisser. It was a beauty."

The blushing began, and she turned to the much safer Matthew. Then it suddenly occurred to her that Jim was flirting with her. It had to work both ways, didn't it? *He* was flirting with *her!*

Her gratified smile faltered as she focused on Matt. He was winking at her. That wasn't even in the flirting manual, but it seemed like it should be. She winked back at him.

His reaction was odd, though. He shook his head, stared hard at Jim's hands, then winked at her again, hard.

"What?" she asked.

His lips tightened and he stared once more at Jim's hands.

"Huh?" Jim asked. "Who did you say what to?"

She followed Matt's gaze and watched as Jim brought his glass slowly to his mouth. Then she saw it. A black bug, a big black bug that looked suspiciously like...

She raised her hand and touched her right eye. The false eyelash was gone. But she knew just where it was.

The glass touched Jim's lips.

# Chapter Four

Matt saw the panic hit Sara's eyes. She'd finally gotten his signals, but it was too late. Jim was already drinking. But he hadn't swallowed the lash yet. Matt had to move, now.

"Stop!" he yelled.

Jim did. Right in the middle of a swallow. Matt glanced to his right and saw that everyone else had, too. The whole room looked as if they were playing Red Light, Green Light. There was no time to enjoy the sight, though. He grabbed Jim's drink out of his hand and tossed the contents into a nearby plant.

"What the hell?" Jim's mouth hung open in shock. His hand hadn't even come down.

Sara was almost as surprised, but he saw the gratitude in her dark brown eyes. She took a deep breath, the first one in a while, he would guess.

"There was a bug," he said calmly, turning back to Jim. "In your drink."

"Jeez, man. You nearly gave me a heart attack. I think I would have preferred the bug."

"It was pretty big. Nasty looking."

"Uh, thanks, I think."

"Why don't you go get another one," Matt said. "I'll keep Sara company."

The look he received from his buddy was as much of a reward as any man could want. He'd think about it during long, dry meetings. The confusion wasn't even the best part. It was the total certainty in his friend's eyes that he'd lost his mind. But it worked. Jim left.

"Thank you."

He turned to Sara, forgetting Jim and the look in an instant. "You might want to take the other one off," he said. "For balance."

She gave the left false lash a delicate pull, then put it in her napkin. "I think I'd better leave now," she said. "Before something else goes wrong."

"Don't," he said, surprising himself with his vehemence. She was a suspect, right? That's all.

Her smile was gracious, and a little sad. "You're right. I should stay until everyone clears out. It'll be safer that way."

He shook his head. "That's not what I meant at all."

Her brow furrowed as she studied him carefully. "I don't mean to be rude, but why are you being so nice to me? Of all people, I would think you would want to keep your distance."

He took a drink to stall her, to think of a reasonable response. He couldn't tell her the truth, naturally. He put his drink down and stared at the glass for a minute, feeling her gaze on him. "I don't know many people out here," he said, not willing to meet that gaze. "You seemed friendly."

She laughed. It was a sound he could get used to. Light, not too high, filled with genuine humor. "They're serving macaroni and cheese tomorrow. I could dump that in your lap if you'd like."

He fought a grin. "No, that's okay. I think we're past that."

"Well, don't say I never offered."

The grin won. "It's a deal." He looked up then, and he was taken aback by his reaction to her smile. It pulled on him with a gentle tug that made him want to get closer. It was innocent and real. Innocent.

He leaned back and turned toward the milling crowd. "Who's the gent with your friend?"

"With Juliet? That's her husband, Armand. He's a poet."

"I've never met a poet before."

"He's very sweet. His accent is stronger than Juliet's, if you can believe that. But he adores her. They've been married over thirty years."

Matt shook his head. "That's a rare thing."

"Isn't that sad?"

He looked at Sara again. She seemed too young to understand the kind of commitment a long marriage required. Yet there was something old-fashioned about her that might mean... No. She wouldn't get serious for a long while. Maybe after marriage number one. But not yet.

"I didn't mean for you to take it so seriously," she said. "It's not *that* sad."

He snapped out of his reverie, surprised and annoyed that he'd let his guard down. "Can I get you another drink?"

She shook her head. "Did I say something wrong? I have a habit of doing that."

"No, not at all. I was just wool-gathering."

She blinked, and tilted her head a bit to the left. She reminded him of a puzzled puppy.

"It's an old expression. It means I was daydreaming."

"Ah," she said, nodding. "That's one I never heard."

"You didn't grow up here, did you?"

"No, I was raised in Switzerland. At a convent school. I got a good education, but my social skills turned out all wrong. At least for this century. I would have fit right into the 1890s. But I can serve a mean tea. I know just what finger to lift when I sip."

"That might come in real handy someday."

She grinned. "Right. All those etiquette emergencies that are on the news so often."

Matt heard Jim approach, which was a relief. He needed the distraction. Sara reminded him too much of Kelly, at least the Kelly he'd known in college. She'd been innocent, too. In the beginning.

"Is it safe to sit down?" Jim asked, as he held his glass for Matt to see. "You want to check my drink for bugs?"

"Looks good to me," Matt said.

Jim slid into the booth next to Sara. Her posture changed instantly. Matt could see the tension in her hands, and in her strained smile. So she really was interested in Forester. Now why should that bother him?

Sara was afraid to move. She'd been a regular Typhoid Mary around Jim, and it was getting ridiculous. If she did one more stupid thing, the game would be over.

There was still a chance that this thing was working. Hadn't he touched her arm, just like in step three? He'd made eye contact, too. Step two. If Juliet was to be believed, those were both important signs, indicating that there was interest. So it was her job to capitalize on her victories.

On the other hand, he might have touched her arm to keep her from spilling something. Looked deep in her eyes to check for insanity.

But she'd give herself the benefit of the doubt. Which meant she had to do something. Now, while she had his attention. Step twenty-one. That was relatively simple, and safe. "I like your hair," she said.

Both men stared at her, and she got the uncomfortable impression that she'd messed things up again. Had they been talking? Or was hair a taboo subject with men?

"Thanks," Jim said. "I like yours, too."

She smiled brightly, then turned away to regroup. Twenty-one had bombed. Maybe she should go with fourteen. That one seemed simple enough. Make prolonged eye contact with a slightly devious smile. Piece of cake.

She waited this time, instead of barging in on their conversation. Jim was talking about his golf game. Matt was listening, but his gaze kept shifting from Jim to her. That was probably in self-defense. He had to keep up his guard.

Better to pay attention to her target. She leaned toward Jim, trying to look as fascinated as humanly possible.

"I tried that new iron, but it didn't feel right, you know?" Jim said. "I need something more substantial. Something with some weight..."

He caught her looking, and her expression must have been perfect, because he lost his train of thought. Bingo! She had eye contact.

Now for the devious smile. She lifted her right brow, just like Scarlett O'Hara had when she wanted something from Rhett. Then she turned up the corners of her mouth. Not much. Just a bit. She wished she'd practiced this in the mirror, but Jim seemed captivated. It must be working.

"Should I call a doctor?" he said, his voice hushed with concern.

She gave up. Her brow came down, and so did the corners of her mouth. "No, no," she said with a sigh. "You couldn't afford the kind of doctor I need. I'll go home now. Do you mind?"

He stared at her for another few seconds, and she was certain he was thinking of padded walls and lithium. Finally though, he moved, scooting out of the booth to let her pass.

Matt got out, too, and both men watched her carefully. She had the feeling she could crow like a rooster right now and they would both nod sagely with that same look in their eyes.

"Thank you," she said, first to Matt, then to Jim. "Please, sit down. I'll be fine."

"Are you sure?" Matt asked. "I can walk you out."

"No. I mean, yes, I'm sure."

"But—"

"I'd really appreciate you sitting down now. Please?"

He gave her a smile that saved a bit of her dignity. It seemed genuine, and for that she was grateful.

Holding on to that feeling, she made her way toward the exit. It didn't surprise her that the crowd parted for her, clearing the way. Everyone but Juliet, of course. She smiled and gave Sara a thumbs-up. Which was rather amusing, given the circumstances.

One thing was clear. The flirting lessons in her book were way too advanced for the likes of her. What she needed was a primer. *See Jane Flirt.*

At least she could still laugh.

MATT LEFT THE PARTY shortly after Sara, and headed for a quick trip to the gym in his apartment building. Of course he was alone, that's the way he liked it. He went through his routine methodically, by the numbers. That part of his Navy training would never leave him, he supposed. Just like the way he made his bed. Every once in a while he tested himself by tossing a quarter onto the sheets. The high bounce inevitably gave him great satisfaction.

What wasn't routine were his thoughts about Sara. He was tempted to write her off as a nut, but her presentation at work shot that one out of the water. It was possible that she was nuts except when it came to Tiny Tina dolls, sort of like Rainman and math, but that didn't ring true, either.

Basically she confused the hell out of him. Her actions weren't consistent with any thief he'd ever dealt with, or any spy. Of course her actions weren't generally consistent with any normal person. What was that look she'd given Jim about? The roving brow, the goofy grin? It wasn't a come-on. At least he didn't think so.

He finished with the weights, and moved over to the treadmill. His thoughts turned to his muscles and his breathing for a while, until he got into a groove. Then Sara came back, like a bad penny.

A very pretty bad penny.

Actually she wasn't the most beautiful woman he'd ever seen. Probably not even in the top ten.

Top twenty? Maybe. She'd gone up a few notches with that slinky dress of hers. He'd never thought about her figure until tonight. But she had one, all right. That was just one more thing that confused him. Why hide that body under all those puritan skirts? And why that black dress tonight? If she'd wanted to stay in the background, she would have stuck to her ordinary wardrobe. She certainly wouldn't have worn those false eyelashes. So why did she want to get noticed?

He stopped running, and the treadmill threw him backward so he banged into the wall behind him. Jim. It had to be. She was after Forester. Just like all the other single women at the plant. He had to give Sara credit. She did stand out. Maybe she wasn't so innocent after all.

He rubbed his shoulder as he turned off the machine. This new theory seemed to hold water, except of course for the spaghetti incident.

Matt suddenly felt exhausted. He got his towel and left the gym, locking up behind him. It was well after midnight, and his brain wasn't in high gear. All this thinking about Sara and Jim was off base. He was distracted from his main focus, the prototypes. Bottom line, Sara Cabot was acting out of character. Therefore, something was wrong. His job was to find out what—without getting emotionally involved. He could do that. He'd done it for years.

"DON'T SAY IT. I don't want to hear that you're quitting. Because you're not."

"I wasn't going to say any such thing." Sara put her purse in her bottom drawer, then turned back to Juliet. "Despite the fact that I'm the biggest klutz in recorded history, I think it *is* working."

Juliet smiled. "Of course it is. But I'm curious. What makes you think so?"

Sara leaned forward. "He touched me. Upper arm. There was even a meaningful look. Eye contact. Just like you said."

"I see."

"And I asked him questions about himself, and it was like magic. He couldn't wait to tell me everything. It's true, he is his favorite topic."

"He's a man. It follows."

Sara moved her stapler until it was even with her tissue box. "But it's funny," she said. "Matt Quartermain wasn't like that. He sort of seemed interested in me. I mean he asked about my schooling. He told me he was at yesterday's meeting because he thought I was friendly."

"Oh?"

"Now what is that tone about? I'm just making an observation."

"I'm just saying, oh."

"I know your *ohs*. They mean a lot more than just oh."

"Oh, really?"

Sara pointed. "See? That's just what I mean."

Juliet laughed. "All right. You've caught me. My

oh was interested. Tell me more about Quartermain.''

Flushed from her small victory, Sara turned to her computer and booted up. ''He saved me last night.''

''From what?''

''Your little makeover. One of my false eyelashes, which I'll never wear again, thank you very much, fell into Jim's drink. Matt got rid of it for me, before Jim gagged on it.''

''That was very gallant.''

Sara's fingers stilled over her keyboard. ''Yes, it was. I hadn't thought of it that way, but you're right. He was very gallant.''

''I see.''

''He was gallant about the spaghetti, too.'' She turned to her friend. ''Why do you think that is?''

''Perhaps he's a gentleman.''

''Hmm. Yes. He is polite.''

''They're not the same thing, *chérie*.''

''No?''

Juliet shook her head. ''One can be polite and not be a gentleman, although a gentleman is always polite.''

''And the difference is?''

''Motivation.''

''You've lost me.''

''A man can be polite when he's stealing your purse. A gentleman would never rest until he got that purse back.''

''You're a regular French Confucius.''

Juliet got up and walked over to Sara's desk. "Thank you, I think.

"Now, what does all this mean, in terms of last night?" Sara swung her chair around so that she was face-to-face with Juliet, who had settled on the small couch.

"I don't know what it means. Except that your lessons are even more successful than we'd planned. But perhaps in a different direction."

"What?" Sara shook her head. "You don't think... He's so... Matthew Quartermain? No."

"Why not?"

That one stopped her. She knew why not, but putting it into words wasn't so easy. "He's, well... With Jim, if it all fell apart, you could move on, you know? It wouldn't be fun, but it wouldn't be deadly."

"And with Matt?"

She sighed and leaned back into her chair. "I think it would be very hard to get Matthew Quartermain to fall in love with a girl. And if he did, and it fell apart, I don't think that girl would get over it. Ever."

The door opened, and Elliot, the Federal Express man, walked in. "Who wants to sign for this?" he asked, holding up a brown package.

Juliet pointed at Sara. "That girl."

# Chapter Five

She couldn't delay any longer. She'd rehearsed so many times, she was confusing herself. Squaring her shoulders, Sara turned the corner and walked up to Jim Forester's door. She lifted her hand to knock, then put it down again.

This wasn't even a hard one. All she had to do was apologize for the champagne mess, and smile. Look around the room and notice predominant colors, or style, or a clue to his hobbies. Get him talking about his likes and dislikes. Minor stuff, no brainers, easy as pie.

She tried again to knock, but hesitated once more. Was it really wise to bring up the champagne calamity? Why put herself in a bad light? No, maybe she should just tell him it had been nice talking to him at the party. Yeah, that's it. She smiled, and went to knock, this time for real. Three short raps. Mission accomplished.

"Finally. I was getting worried there."

The voice, Jim's voice, came from behind her.

She turned slowly. How long had he been watching? His smile suggested that he'd been there for a long time.

"I was just…I didn't know… Oh, hell."

He laughed, and stepped next to her to open the door. "Come on in, Sara. I promise, there aren't any lions in my den."

He didn't leave her any room to run, so she did as he asked. Her blush didn't even last too long. Maybe she *was* becoming immune.

"Have a seat. I have to make a call, then I'll be right with you."

She nodded while she did a quick scan of the room. Juliet had said she'd find a lot of information if she looked for it, and darn if she wasn't right. There was a lot of Jim in the decor, even though it was quite businesslike and a little formal.

She settled into one of the leather club chairs facing him, while he sat in his big executive chair behind his highly polished teak desk. The desk was tidy, with only a notebook computer, a company mug and a few papers on it. The real clues were on top of the low filing cabinets and on the walls.

The predominant theme seemed to be testosterone. Manly colors, dark green mostly, with a little tartan plaid here and there, set off by the dichotomy of three baby dolls propped up on one set of shelves. Next to Precious Patty was a gun, an old-fashioned one, mounted like a trophy. Okay, he liked guns. A hobby she couldn't relate to, but then she'd never tried.

He smiled at her as he said something about shipping dates into the phone, then his gaze went to his computer. She swung around to check out the other side of the room. There were some pictures on that wall, one with Jim and Ralph and Lilly Marsh at last year's company picnic. Then there was a photo of Jim in hunting gear. Camouflage. He liked to play soldier? Well, okay. Guys are just different, that's all. Hadn't Juliet told her that many times?

Her gaze traveled back to the man in question, and she tried to reconcile his love for shooting things with his impeccable style in the office. He really did look stunning, like a model for *GQ*. His suit was charcoal gray, fit him like a dream and set off his blond Robert Redford looks.

He sat back in his chair with the easy confidence of a man with the world on a string. She waited for some butterflies to flutter in her tummy, but it didn't happen. She felt a bit hungry, but that was it. Why not? Wasn't he the acknowledged lust-bunny of the whole company? Hadn't she always sighed when he walked by? So why now, when it mattered, did he do nothing to stir her libido? Nerves?

He turned his back to her, so she was able to size up his rear, so to speak. She appreciated the broad shoulders, and could well imagine that his bottom was quite nice, although even Jim Forester would have to go a far distance to outdo the Federal Express man.

While he continued looking out his window, Sara took the opportunity to do a little desk scouting. There wasn't much there to scout, except for his file, which, she saw after turning her head to the right, was marked Personal. Dare she? No, it was too much. That would be snooping, not scouting. But Juliet had told her, "All's fair in love and war," and that there was no such thing as being too sneaky when the object was matrimony. Or at the very least a date.

Before she could think more about it, she opened the file. Panic struck immediately, and she closed it before she could see anything inside. She didn't care if all was fair. She wasn't a snoop.

Jim turned around shortly after that, and she looked at the dolls while she calmed down.

"So, what can I do for the fair Sara today?" he asked.

She hadn't noticed him finish his call, and she didn't feel quite ready. "I just wanted to say I was sorry about that champagne thing last night. I'll be happy to pay for the dry cleaning. It really was all my fault, and your tie is green, isn't it?"

He blinked. "Yes, it is green. And no, don't worry about the champagne."

"So green is your favorite color?"

He blinked again. "I guess so. I hadn't thought about it."

"How do you feel about music?"

"I like it?"

She nodded, getting into the swing of things. "All kinds? Classical? Jazz?"

"I like jazz. Rock. Not country. Is this a test? Am I passing?"

"No, it's not a test, per se. I just don't know you very well, and I'd like to."

He smiled, and settled back in his chair. "I see. I'd like to get to know you, too. But let's skip the favorite colors and get to some more interesting questions."

She crossed her legs and sat all the way back. "Like what?"

"Well, we can start with your choice in clothes. How come you always hide that lovely figure of yours? What are you afraid of?"

She looked down at her dress. It was one of her favorites. Pastel flowers on a background of soft cream, it flowed around her when she walked. It was on the large side, but that was the style. "I don't mean to hide anything."

"Oh, but you do. You surprised me last night with that little black number. I got the message."

"There wasn't a message. Honest."

He lifted his right brow and smiled seductively. Just as she'd tried to do last night. He was much better at this flirting thing than she was.

"How about you and I go to dinner tonight?" he

said softly. "Then I can find out all about your favorite colors."

"Oh, uh, dinner? Hmm. Dinner."

"You know, the meal after lunch?"

"Perfume?"

"Huh?" He was blinking again.

"I was just curious. If you had one you liked especially. Or maybe not. Never mind." She stood up, and started backing her way to the door.

"Obsession."

"What?"

"The perfume. I like Obsession."

She nodded, taking another step out. Juliet would kill her if she found out she'd passed on his invitation to dinner. But she wasn't ready. Not yet.

"What about tonight?" he said.

"I think I'm busy, but I'll have to check. I'll get back to you. About dinner." She turned, ready for her getaway. Only someone blocked her path. Not someone. Matthew Quartermain.

"Dinner?" he said. "It's just lunchtime. Hi, Sara. I was coming to ask Jim to join me. Why don't you come along, too?"

"Oh, no. I think that would be a mistake."

"I brought a change of clothes to work. Just in case."

His smile awakened the dormant butterflies in her stomach. Big time. But that was surely just nerves.

"So what have we got to lose, right? Come on. I'll treat."

"If you're treating," Jim said, "I don't want to go to the cafeteria."

"Too bad. That's the offer. Take it or leave it."

Sara actually felt the tension in her shoulders ease. Once the conversation wasn't focused on her, it was actually easy to be with these two men. They were good enough friends to tease each other, and that was something she was comfortable with. No pressure, just friendship.

That's where she'd gone wrong, she decided. She'd been putting too much pressure on herself. She didn't have to make Jim fall madly in love with her. At least not yet. She could begin with friendship. The idea struck her as a eureka moment, right up there with the discovery of fire.

"Okay, I'm ready," she said.

Matt looked at her with wide eyes. "You are, huh?"

She nodded. "Yes."

"I don't want to disappoint you. Maybe we should go to a restaurant."

"No, really, it's fine."

Jim came around his desk and joined them at the door. They walked toward the lunchroom, the men on either side of her. She felt short.

"So, Matt. What's your favorite color?"

Matt turned to Jim with a puzzled look. "What?"

"Sara wants to know, don't you?"

She supposed this was just gentle teasing, but it made her a bit uncomfortable. Jim was such a new person to her that she found it hard to find the line between teasing and making fun. But then she was so sensitive now, after all her mistakes. "Yes, I do. I think it says something about a person."

Matt turned his confused look to her. "Favorite color, huh? I don't know that I've ever given that a moment's thought."

She tugged at his sleeve and pulled him closer to avoid hitting a mail cart. His chest pressed against her arm, and she was startled at how hard he was. As if he was made of something other than flesh and blood. Iron, maybe. Then he moved away, and they walked into the cafeteria.

Jim stood aside to let her get in line first. She grabbed her tray and headed down the line, looking not for food she liked, but for food that wouldn't shake, stain, drip, spill or dribble. She decided on fish sticks and crackers. Not the most appealing lunch, but certainly the safest. The odd thing, though, was how people kept saying hello to her.

Most everyone she knew was friendly, in a company sort of way, but today they were practically chummy. It took her quite some time to figure out that they were all waiting for another show. Another disaster. She'd hate to disappoint so many, but she was bound and determined to shake off her jinx and start acting like a normal, cautious adult.

Matt paid for all three lunches, as he'd promised, then led them to the table. She successfully moved her plate from the tray to the Formica without spilling a drop. Even taking her seat was accomplished easily. For once, she felt in the clear.

"Red," Matt said. "No, wait. Blue."

She nodded, then looked at Jim. "Red is a power color. It's somewhat aggressive, but mostly it indicates someone who won't be pushed around." Then she turned to Matt. "Blue is more passive, but it's still strong. It's a more peaceful color, one that leads to meditation and contemplation. The combination is really quite stable."

Matt smiled. "Stable, huh? Okay. I can deal with that." He pointed to Jim. "What were his colors?"

"Green," she said. "Dark green."

"Green probably stands for potency, right?" Jim said.

She nodded. "To some degree, yes. But it's also about life, rebirth and nature."

Jim seemed pleased. "She also wanted to know what music I like. And what perfume—"

"You wear?" Matt said.

"I like on women."

This was better. Light conversation, the topic something she knew about. The teasing was even on a level she could deal with without become flustered. That's what drove her crazy about this whole flirting experiment. In most areas of her life, she was reasonably sure of her footing. But when it came to interactions of the sexual kind, she felt like such a rube.

"So?" Jim waited on Matt.

"Jeez, if I'd known there was going to be a test, I would have studied."

"It's not a test, per se," Jim said, repeating her words to him. "She just doesn't know you very well, and she'd like to." He grinned at her, but she wasn't quite sure if his teasing was gentle or not. She turned back to Matt. "That's right," she said. "It's just exploration."

"Okay, okay." He thought for a long moment, then said, "I like the scent of soap on a woman. No adornments. Clean, fresh. Simple."

She felt her face warm, and she looked at the remains of her fish sticks. With Jim, she knew the innuendos were there, that his undertone was sexual, and although it wasn't easy, she was trying to deal with that. But Matt confused her. She didn't think he was saying anything spicy, not overtly, but she kept interpreting his words that way. If only she had the experience that would help her know if what she heard was what he meant. Or something.

Sara heard the click of the PA system being turned on. The room stilled as Mr. Marsh's voice boomed all over the plant.

"Ladies and gentlemen, the reports are in for the quarter. Productivity is up three percent and sales are up eleven percent."

Most everyone clapped at that, but stilled quickly as Marsh continued. "However. We had two accidents within the past three months, both due to carelessness. We need to work on that, people. But, all in all, well done. As always, I'm open to all ideas for improvement. Thank you very much.''

The din immediately picked up where it had left off. Sara remembered times when Marsh's announcements had brought uneasy quiet to the lunchroom. When people were afraid for their jobs. But that hadn't happened in a long while.

''I'm still waiting on an answer about dinner,'' Jim said.

She turned his way. He was certainly persistent. She should just say yes. Wasn't a date the point of this whole thing? But she couldn't. He was moving too fast. The way he smiled at her made her think of the Big Bad Wolf looking at Red Riding Hood.

Besides, he knew this kind of thing didn't come naturally to her. She honestly believed he wasn't being malicious in any way, but she wasn't sure she could keep up with him. The ice felt too thin, and she was walking with heavy boots.

''Instead of dinner, why don't we meet in the park tomorrow?'' she said. ''We could take a walk.''

He looked down and absently tugged his right ear. ''The park?''

She nodded. ''You know. The one on Fourth. With the big pond. It's very pretty there now.''

Matt chuckled, and once again, she knew she'd done something wrong. But what?''

Jim nodded. ''Sure. The park is fine.''

''Ten o'clock?''

''Sure.'' He looked at his watch, swallowed the

last of his soda, then stood. "You kids finish up. I've got to run." He put his hand on Sara's shoulder and gave it a gentle squeeze. "Ten in front of the pond, right?"

"By the concession stand."

"Got it." With that he headed for the door, and as Sara watched his progress, she couldn't help but notice the many gazes that followed him out.

Matt didn't need to look around to know that every eye, well at least every feminine eye, was on Jim. He didn't care. What did bother him was watching Sara watch Jim. Which was a difficult notion, especially tough when he remembered his objective. It was getting harder for him to think of Sara as the company thief.

She was entirely too innocent. Just look at how she was going about getting Jim to notice her. It wasn't smooth, or practiced. It was paint-by-numbers flirting.

On the other hand, she'd done nothing concrete to dispel the notion that she could be involved with the piracy. The issue of blackmail was still out there, and until he could logically, physically, prove that Sara had nothing to do with the stolen prototypes, he was obliged to keep a watch on her. He supposed that would be made easier now that she was after Jim. But he didn't like it. Not one bit.

"You laughed," she said.

"What?"

"A few moments ago." She looked at him seriously, as if he were a puzzle she was trying to figure out. "When I mentioned the park."

"Oh, well, that was nothing."

"No, come on. It amused you. Why?"

He couldn't keep looking at her. She did something to his brain that made it hard to focus. Instead he concentrated on his Salisbury steak. "Jim, at the park? It's hard to imagine."

"Why do you say that?"

He shrugged, then took a drink of his soda. "No reason. Forget it."

She reached over and touched his forearm. He could barely feel her fingertips through his suit and his shirt; it was more of a hint than a reality. But it was enough to make him completely lose his train of thought. It was her nails. Soft, curved, white with perfect pink moons. Her hands. Delicate, small on his arm, lovely. Her wrist. He could encircle that wrist with his hand and still have room to spare. He could break her, but all he wanted to do was protect her.

She moved her hand away, and he looked up to see that she was still studying him, but now there was an element of fear in her confused gaze. Just a hint, an acknowledgment that something had just happened between them, and she had no idea what.

"I have to go," she said.

"Not yet."

She looked from his eyes to his mouth, then back again. He watched in silent fascination as her cheeks warmed with a pink flush. Her lips parted slightly, as if she needed a little more air to breathe. Kissing those lips became his only thought. Kissing them, and taking the rest of her breath away.

He leaned toward her. She stilled, except for the rise and fall of her chest.

He inched closer until he could feel the heat of her, and then a laugh, as sharp as breaking glass, woke him. He sat up straight, turned away from Sara and her spell. He cleared his throat, acutely aware that he'd made a public display that was totally unacceptable.

Without another look her way, he stood up. "Excuse me," he said, aware that the gruffness of his tone had more to do with what she'd done to him than his current embarrassment.

Although he wanted to hurry, he forced himself to walk casually, to glance at his co-workers, to smile. He couldn't let them see that he'd been thrown for a loop, that a woman like Sara could make him lose his head. Especially a woman like Sara. He'd been down that road before, and it had ended in utter humiliation. Kelly's innocence had trapped him in her lacy web, and he'd been left there to die. And here he was walking right into the same trap again.

He nearly made a clean getaway. But he looked back, just for a second. Sara's gaze was on him, simple, sweet, confused. This wouldn't be easy. He'd have to keep his guard up twenty-four hours a day. Because that look had the power to bring him to his knees.

Sara watched him leave and remembered how to breathe. She wasn't sure what had just happened. It must have had something to do with the lights in the room dimming, or the sudden lack of oxygen. Or maybe she'd developed an allergy to fish sticks. But when she looked at her arms, there were no hives.

He hadn't answered her question, she realized. At the time, it hadn't mattered. All that she cared about, during those few seconds when the world stopped, was that he was close to her.

She quickly went over her flirting steps, trying to recall if there was anything about stopping time, but there wasn't. Gathering her belongings quickly, she headed out of the lunchroom. This was a problem for Juliet. Surely she'd know what was going on.

Thankfully Juliet was at her desk when Sara got to the office. She told her friend what had occurred, waiting for a logical explanation. But Juliet failed her.

"Just keep doing what you're doing, Sara," she said.

"But what about Matthew?"

Juliet nodded sagely. "Don't worry about him. You have a date tomorrow with Jim, yes?"

Sara nodded. "At the park."

"And do you remember what you're supposed to bring?"

She nodded again. "But—"

"Trust me. It's all going according to the plan. You have nothing to worry about."

Sara went to her desk and looked at her computer screen. The numbers there blurred together. "I don't understand," she said.

"You will."

"When?"

"Soon, *chérie*. Soon."

Sara sighed. "You scare me sometimes, you know that?"

"That's well and good," Juliet said. "I scare you because I'm telling you the truth. There's nothing to fear. But everything to hope for."

"Unless I mess up again."

"That's not likely, is it? I think the worst is over, and everything will run smoothly from now on."

Sara smiled at her friend. "Your optimism is— is—"

"Inspiring?"

"Delusional."

# Chapter Six

Matt felt like a heel. Here he was at the park, waiting for Sara, and she didn't even know Jim wasn't going to show. Matt felt sure that the moment Sara caught sight of him, she'd be utterly disappointed. She'd be too polite to say anything, but he'd see it in the set of her shoulders, the tilt of her mouth, the sadness in her eyes. He still wasn't sure if she was involved in the office piracy, so his presence here made good security sense, but he did know that Sara was attracted to Jim, not him.

They were such opposites that it wasn't conceivable that Sara could be pleased with the switch. She was going after Forester, and he had no business getting in the way. He wouldn't have come today, except for his conversation with Jim.

Forester said that while he'd turned his back on her for a few seconds, Sara had snuck a peek at some private papers on his desk.

Matt knew for a fact that Sara's good breeding was inconsistent with snooping, so she had to have a reason for going through Jim's file. Maybe she was looking for passwords?

It was his job, dammit. He had to investigate this. It had nothing to do with how good she smelled, how pretty she was, how her eyes went wide with wonder. She was a suspect, that's all. Nothing more, nothing less.

He got up from the bench and paced back and forth. He was in the mood for a run. His nerves were on edge, his temper short. He needed to expend energy, and soon.

The park had gotten crowded in the last half hour. Kids were throwing Frisbees and softballs, kites were being readied for flight, boom boxes were being tuned to battling stations. But he didn't see Sara. Maybe she'd backed out of the deal, too.

He took a turn at the water fountain, then headed back to the bench. That's when he saw her. She was running, but he didn't think that's what she'd had in mind.

A dog, a really huge dog, a Great Dane that probably outweighed her by fifty pounds, was pulling her along behind him. Sara looked wild-eyed, and he could hear her yell, "Whoa!" from the other side of the walkway.

It was quite a spectacle, and it would have been funny if he didn't know that there was no way that little bit of a woman was going to stop that big bruiser of a dog. He set off to intercept.

He headed straight for the black-and-white dog,

making a mental note to try to avoid the slobbering tongue that waggled with each lope. "Let go of the leash," he yelled.

Either she didn't hear him, or panic had set in, because she held on for dear life.

Matt ran full-out just as the dog swerved to avoid a bench. Matt went one way, the dog another. Sara was headed down the middle, and she was in for a spill.

He turned as quickly as he could, racing to reach her before she took a header, but the dog's trajectory saved her in the nick of time. Then Matt was chasing the two of them, Sara still yelling, "Whoa, boy! Stop!"

He yelled, "Drop the leash," even though he knew it was useless. A kid stepped in front of him, and he swerved to the left. A garbage can made him turn to the right. It was like being back with the SEALs, on an obstacle course. Except civilians were involved here, and he wanted no casualties. Especially not Sara.

He ran faster when he got a clean shot, and it was a good thing, because the dog was headed straight for the pond. Matt was surprised at how fast he had to go to catch them. It didn't seem possible she could run as quickly as that. But finally, he did catch her. He ran next to her, keeping the pace, and grabbed on to the leash.

Only Sara didn't let go.

"I've got it!" he yelled.

"I can't let go!"

"Why not?"

"It's not my dog!"

He looked at her. And then he tripped over a skateboard. He went down hard. He didn't even have the presence of mind to tuck and roll. His stomach hit first, and the air left him in a whoosh. His chin hit next, slamming his mouth shut so hard it vibrated. He lay there stunned for a moment, but Sara's yelps got him moving before he'd regained his breath.

They were at the pond's edge when he started running again. The dog had mercifully slowed in order to bark at the ducks, but his intention was clear. If he kept going, and Sara didn't let go, they'd both be swimming.

Matt could breathe again, if only in great gasps, and years of training let him count on his muscles to do what had to be done. He reached Sara's side quickly and grabbed hold of the leash. He pulled back with all the strength he had, which got the dog's attention.

The Great Dane turned abruptly and headed toward them, the ducks forgotten for the moment. As Matt tried to peel Sara's hands from the leather leash, the dog slammed into his side in an unwelcome friendly greeting. It was more important to free Sara than it was to pet the pooch, but it wasn't easy. She was holding on with both hands, so hard her knuckles were white.

"Let go," he said. "I've got him."

"He's Sirius."

"I know he's serious. He's out to kill you."

"No, I mean his name is Sirius. Like the dog star."

He looked at her again, simply astonished at her priorities. "I don't care what his name is. *Let go!*"

She did.

He saw what the leash had done to her hands. The soft white pads of flesh were red and angry, with bitter deep grooves cutting into her palm and fingers.

His examination was cut short however, when the dog bumped him again, and then he felt the leash dig into his legs. Too late, he looked down to see that Sirius had circled them not once, not twice, but three times. Matt grabbed for his collar, but the dog was too far away, and he couldn't move his legs to go after him.

"Oh, dear," Sara said, as the Great Dane headed once more for the pond.

Matt's comment was far less delicate.

"We're going to drown, aren't we?" she asked him.

He nodded. "Yep."

"It was nice of you to try to help."

They were pulled, as a unit, behind the dog, who didn't seem to mind the extra weight. As a matter of fact, he seemed to take it as a challenge, putting all his considerable strength into the task.

They shuffled forward, the awkward position making it hard to gain a foothold. Matt was plastered against Sara from calf to shoulder, and her face was inches from his. Wrapped like a birthday present and closer than twins, Matt's body decided to react to the intimacy in a most ungentlemanly fashion.

"Ow. Wait. Stop."

He could feel Sara's efforts to slow the progression toward their demise, which made his problem grow. Then she looked up at him, which was easy with her face so close to his. "What's that?"

He swallowed, digging his heels into the grass.

Her eyes got wide. Really, really wide. "Oh!"

Okay, so drowning wasn't such a bad way to go. John Paul Jones had done it, and he was considered a hero. "Just stop moving," he said.

"I'm not doing it on purpose!"

They hit the water's edge, while Matt tried to think of others who had died by drowning. Sara kept squirming, despite his request. The spectators were yelling now, helpfully suggesting that they stop fooling around and get out of the water. Matt wanted to hurt someone.

Sirius seemed to be after one particular duck. The duck farthest from the shore. Any second, Matt felt sure they would hit a dip and plunge down into the icy cold. He wondered if anyone at all would try to save them. Or if they would just continue to shout suggestions from the sidelines.

"I'm sorry," Sara said, her voice quivery.

"That's okay. It's not your fault we're in this mess."

"But it is."

"Why? Did you train your dog to do this trick?"

"No," she said, her voice high as they went another foot deeper into the lake. "I was trying to impress you. Well, Jim. I wanted him to see how good I was with pets."

"What?"

They went a few steps farther in. Now the water was up to his waist. The cold had done one good thing. He was no longer saluting the flag. "Next time," he said, "try it with a hamster."

She giggled.

Everything was so damned absurd, he couldn't help but laugh, too.

They kept going farther and farther into the lake, but the water didn't get deeper. She was truly cracking up now, and when he saw the tears fall from the corners of her eyes, he laughed harder. Then he became aware of how her breasts jiggled against his chest, and he wasn't laughing anymore.

It took him several seconds to realize that something had changed. That someone had joined them in the lake.

A man, a park guard, was standing waist-deep in water, right next to Sirius. He reached over with a slow steady hand, and unclipped the leash from the dog's collar. Then, he walked over to Matt, Sirius trotting obediently at his side, and said, "This here's a family park, mister. Try your kinky stuff down-town.''

Sara burst out laughing again, and Matt couldn't keep it together. He tried to untangle them, but it didn't go smoothly. He just couldn't seem to get it together. Every time he tried to stop, he'd feel her chest against him, her laughter a physical thing, and he'd lose it once more.

Finally, finally, he unwound the leash until there was nothing pressing them together. Yet he didn't move. She didn't move. He no longer heard the crowd.

"You're all wet," he said.

"So are you."

"We need to do something about that."

"My apartment's only a few blocks away."

"Then we should go."

"We should."

But they didn't. They stood still, waist-deep in the lake, as close now as when the leash had bound them together. He stared into her eyes, looking, searching for something—he didn't know what. She stared back, her gaze as intent as his own.

It was Sirius who got them moving. The dog barked, startling Sara so much she nearly fell back into the water. Matt grabbed onto her, holding both arms. He pulled her close again, and he didn't stop until his mouth was on hers.

Sara closed her eyes and abandoned herself to his kiss. The pressure grew, and a sudden warmth spread from her chest. She felt his hands on her back, exploring, pulling her closer still, and she mirrored his movements. His back felt impossibly broad and muscled, so masculine and foreign. But it was his kiss that took her breath away.

He was doing things to her she'd never imagined in all her daydreams. Tasting her, filling her, and turning her world upside-down. Again, she mirrored him, finding inexplicable delight in the intimacy, in the soft warmth of his mouth, in the taste of him.

Oh, she'd dreamed of a kiss like this, but her imagination had been stingy. How had she not known that a kiss could change everything? That it would cause a riot of sensations all over her body? That she would never want it to stop?

He pulled away, and she moaned at the loss, then he kissed her neck and that was new and wonderful, too. But not good enough. She reached for his jaw with her hand and gently moved him back to her mouth. He smiled, and obliged.

She was bolder, this time. She pressed him closer, and moved herself against him. She felt his erection again, and this time it didn't embarrass her. It made her feel sexy and powerful, and brought new sensations to the pit of her stomach.

She tasted his lips, and breathed in his scent. He moaned, and she felt the vibrations from his throat.

When he pulled away, she didn't try to stop him. But only because she was dizzy and breathless.

"We need to get out of these clothes," he said.

She nodded, and reached for the bottom of her T-shirt. His hands stopped her. "I didn't mean right here."

She nodded again. "My apartment."

"Your apartment."

He took her hand and they slogged through the water toward the walkway. Once on dry land, she became aware of people around her: little kids, old ladies, a hot dog vendor. When had they appeared?

Her jeans felt plastered on, heavy and itchy and she wanted them off. Her shoes squished loudly with each step. But it was a small price to pay for the bonus of seeing what the water did to Matt's sweatpants. They looked like a relief map of his body, perfect in every detail. She kept stealing glances at his thighs, and slightly above, embarrassing herself each time for her less than noble thoughts, but looking just the same.

Sirius decided he was too soaked, and shook his entire body to rid himself of the water. It worked very well. Water flew everywhere, but mostly all over her. When he finished, he looked at her intently, probably wondering why she didn't shake, too.

"Which way?" Matt asked.

She pointed south. "It's two blocks down."

He took the leash and connected it to Sirius's collar. He didn't let it out much, though, so the three of them could walk as a tight group.

Sara wanted to say something about the kiss. But

she didn't know how. She wanted to know if that was how he kissed everyone, or if that kiss was special for her. She wanted to know if it was natural to react as she had—growing giddy and breathless and weak in the knees, or if that was just a part of kissing when one was an adult. Mostly she wanted to know why she wanted so badly to do it again. Was it the kiss itself? Or the man who'd done the kissing?

She glanced his way, and found him looking at her, but as soon as their eyes met, he looked away. That was her biggest clue yet. If the kiss hadn't been a big deal, he wouldn't have done that, would he? Matthew Quartermain wasn't the type to glance shyly at a woman, unless something was going on. She wished she could speak to Juliet and get her opinion.

Of course, all of this was supposed to have happened with Jim. Jim! She turned to Matt. "What happened to Jim?"

Matt's shoulders sagged noticeably, and she wondered about that. Were he and Jim having words?

"Something came up. He couldn't get in touch with you, so he asked me to come by and give his apologies."

"Oh. Thank you."

"No sweat. I was going to the park anyway. For a run."

"I see."

They got to the street corner and Sirius sat down. He looked up at Matt, waiting for the okay to cross.

"Now, you're trained?" Matt said to him. "What happened back there? Duck dementia?"

Sirius wagged his tail. Matt tugged on his leash and they all crossed the street. Sara smiled.

"Who does this guy belong to?"

"My next-door neighbor. He's really very sweet, you know."

"The neighbor, or the dog?"

"Well, both actually. But I meant Sirius. I guess he just got a little overexcited."

"He's not the only one," Matt said under his breath. But she heard him. Her spirits picked up again. Maybe he wasn't referring to the kiss, but as long as it was open to interpretation, she chose to believe he was. That was part of her flirting book that she didn't have trouble with.

*It never hurts to believe the best,* Juliet had written. *It won't change the outcome, but the waiting will be much more pleasant.*

So if he meant something totally different, she'd find out soon enough. In the meantime, she would be quite content to think that he'd been excited over a kiss with her.

He had gotten that erection, hadn't he? That was something. She couldn't wait to tell Juliet. She'd given a man—no, not just a man—Matthew Quartermain, an erection! It was a good one, too. At least she thought it was. It felt as if it was. She'd read about them, and heard people talk about them, but she'd never actually given one before. A person had to be pretty darn sexy to do that. Especially with someone as strong and as self-possessed as Matt.

She looked at him again, and caught him doing the same to her. Only this time, he didn't look away. She didn't, either. This time she smiled.

Just then Sirius barked and jolted forward, pulling Matt along with him. They'd reached home, and the Great Dane was obviously thrilled. Matt let him go, and the dog raced to his backyard, probably making a beeline for the food bowl.

"I gather this is where you live?" He was looking at her duplex. She lived on the right, and Mrs. Crane lived on the left.

"Let's get you out of those wet things," she said. She got her key out and opened the door.

He hesitated on the step and slipped off his shoes. He placed them neatly in the sun, and she followed his example. They both took off their socks, then entered the apartment.

He looked around, and she was very grateful she'd picked up this morning. Her apartment was a joy to her, and she'd taken great pains to make it comfortable and pretty. The rooms weren't large, but they were big enough for her few things. The couch she'd bought when she got out of college. The rocker that used to belong to her grandmother. The coffee table she'd found at the flea market. And of course there was room for her little things. The pictures of her family, the doilies Aunt Esther made, the antique pitcher filled with dried flowers and especially her family quilt. She watched Matt look around, and when he gave a very quiet little nod, she felt deliciously proud. He approved. Not that it would matter if he didn't. It was her place and she loved it. But it was nice all the same.

"The bathroom is over there," she said, pointing past the kitchen. "Why don't you get out of those things. I'll give you a fresh towel and something to put on while your clothes dry."

He nodded.

"If you want to shower, please do. That lake was none too clean."

He stopped at the door. "What about you?"

"I'll shower a bit later."

He nodded again, and stepped inside. She waited a few seconds, more anxious than ever to change out of her itchy jeans. The door opened, and his hand came out holding his soaking sweats. She took them, forcing herself not to take a peek inside the bathroom.

By the time she'd changed, picked out the only robe she thought would fit him and taken the clothes to the dryer, Matt had finished with his shower.

She knocked once on the door. "I've got your robe."

He stuck his hand out again, and she gave him the garment, not sure at all if he was going to like it. It was a little feminine.

"This is it?" he said.

"It's all I've got."

"I can't wear this."

"It's only for a little while. The clothes are already in the dryer."

"I'll stay in here."

"You can't. I've heated up some soup. It's already getting cold."

There was a long stretch of silence, then the door slowly opened. Matt stood hesitantly inside, wearing a light pink jersey bathrobe with a feathery neckline, cuffs and hem. The robe did fit him around the waist well, but the top gaped open revealing a dark, muscled hairy chest.

She turned away quickly so he wouldn't see her grin.

"One laugh, and I'm out of here," he said, his voice a low growl.

"I'm not laughing," she said. "It's only a robe for heaven's sake. You're not wearing it to the prom."

He grunted, then walked past her into the kitchen.

"Sit down," she said. "Do you want tea? Coffee?"

"Just water. Thank you." He sat at her dining-room table, and she realized for the first time how small it was. It fit her nicely, but a man, especially a man of Matt's height, looked like a giant in the delicate chair. She'd never thought about a man at her table. Not a real man, flesh and blood and muscle.

He tasted the soup she'd quickly heated, and nodded. "This is great."

"Thanks. It's an old recipe I picked up in Switzerland. Onions and herbs."

She got him his water, then sat down across from him. Although she was hungry, she just watched him eat for a while. That was another unexpected pleasure. He really seemed to like her cooking, and he ate with gusto, a sign of good health and vigor.

What was happening here? It was painfully obvious that she was attracted to Matt in a way she wasn't to Jim. But Juliet had picked out the other man, and Juliet had her reasons. She would talk to her friend first thing on Monday. Perhaps there was room for negotiation.

Matt sat back in his chair. "Thanks. I didn't realize how hungry I was."

"Swimming will do that."

He smiled. "Yeah, swimming." He shook his head. "So tell me again why you borrowed the world's largest dog?"

She flushed. "It was nothing. Really."

"No, no. You said you wanted Jim to see how you were with pets?"

She put her spoon down and folded her hands. "Please, can we not talk about that? I'm just not up to any more embarrassment. Can't you just talk to me like...like one of your male friends?"

His grin changed slowly into something a little bit wicked. "Sure, but then we'd have to talk about hooters, and I don't think you'd like that."

"Hooters?"

He laughed. "I forgot. You grew up in Europe. Hooters is a colloquial term for breasts. You know, like melons, or, um…headlights. They're all just terms of endearment from men with no brains."

She frowned. "I see. But 'hooters?' Why?"

"I don't know."

"Is it owl-related? I can't imagine what it's supposed to represent. Melons, okay. I can at least picture that, but hooters?" She looked down at her own chest. Her breasts weren't melon-shaped. They weren't big enough, although she had known one girl in school who would fit the bill. And they definitely didn't look like hooters, whatever they may be.

She looked up at his laughter.

"I've never thought about the origin of the word hooters, but now you've got me curious. I'll have to look into that."

"Let me know your findings, okay?"

He nodded. "Didn't you have nicknames for… parts…when you went to school?"

"Sure. I may have been at a convent school, but I was still curious about all that."

"Did all of the nicknames make sense?"

She thought a moment. "No. Some did. But not all. For example, the blue tulip. I mean, what part of a man could possibly resemble a blue tulip?"

# Chapter Seven

"A blue tulip?" Matt had to turn away from her. He held his laughter in by sheer force of will. How was he going to get out of this one? She was so damn naive, but at the same time, she was intuitive and intelligent. Her attitude was clear enough. She wanted a straight answer to her question. He just didn't know if he was brave enough to give her one.

"Well?"

"Give me a minute," he said, still not able to look at her.

He heard her chair scrape. "I'm sorry. I didn't mean to put you on the spot. I'll go check on the clothes."

He turned. "No, it wasn't that you put me—well, yes, you did, but it isn't bad or anything."

She bowed her head, then slowly raised it again to face him squarely. "Please don't patronize me, Mr. Quartermain. I know I don't have the kind of worldliness I should have at my age. And I know I ask questions that embarrass people. I do it all the time. I don't mean to, but I need to catch up, you see? I'm like someone who's been in a coma for years, and suddenly discovers that while she's been sleeping, the world has grown up. They tried to protect me, but all they did was make me feel out of place everywhere I go.''

He stood and walked close to her. Close enough to touch, but he didn't do that. She took a step back and turned her head.

"Sara," he said softly. He waited until she looked at him again. Her eyes were filled with a sadness that came from somewhere deep inside her. A hurt that was as old as she was.

"I'm not making fun of you, Sara. I wouldn't do that."

She nodded. "I know. It's not you. You've been very nice to me, even when I've been impossible."

"You shouldn't worry so much about catching up. There's a lot to be said for innocence. The world you want to belong to isn't such a nice place."

"I know that, too. And I'm strong enough to deal with it. That's what no one seems to believe. I don't need protection. I need honesty."

He reached over and took her hand in his. "I'll make you a deal. I'll be honest with you, if you'll smile again."

She tried, but he wasn't convinced.

"Okay. You want honesty? You got it. But if you think about it for a moment, I bet you'll figure out the similarities between a tulip—"

She nodded, looked to the left for a moment, then opened her eyes very wide. "Oh."

"Right." He cleared his throat, grateful that she'd gotten the point so quickly.

"And the blue part?"

"Well…"

She shook her head. "Never mind. I can figure that out for myself."

He nodded, relieved beyond words.

She got up on tiptoe and kissed him lightly on the cheek. "Thank you. I know that was uncomfortable, and that we don't know each other well enough to discuss tulips of any color. You've been a gentleman, and you've rescued me more often than I deserve. So I promise. I'll take my questions elsewhere, at least the ones that will make you blush."

"I don't blush," he said with a wink. "I just get suntanned." He squeezed her hand, but instead of the smile he'd expected, she grimaced, and he remembered the damage the leash had done.

Capturing the other hand, too, he brought her palms up for inspection. They were still raw-looking and swollen. "You need to put a cold compress on these," he said. "And some antiseptic where the skin is broken."

"I'll do that," she said. "Thank you."

His gaze moved from her delicate hands to her beautiful face. She was close enough to kiss, and he wanted to do just that. But how could he? Not again. It was unforgivable that he'd kissed her in the pond.

In her house? When he was dressed in this ridiculous piece of fluffery?

She leaned forward, just a smidgen, enough to tell him what her intentions were. All he had to do was bend that last inch. Her mouth opened slightly, and he felt that same rush of heat surge from his groin, that same urge to take her in his arms and not let go.

He wanted to teach her all the things she didn't know.

He stepped back, reeling from the insanity of his own thoughts. This little innocent maiden was a suspect in a major crime. It was clear as hell that she had been flirting big time with Jim Forester over the last week, and that she wanted something from him. Or at least from his files. Now that Jim wasn't here, she was going all soft and trembly in his arms. Innocent? Or too clever by half?

"What's wrong?"

"Nothing. I just thought you wanted to go check on the clothes."

The confusion in her eyes almost convinced him that he was off base. Almost. He went back to the table and sat down, anxious now to get dressed and leave. If he stayed much longer, he might forget again. Forget why he was here, and why Sara Cabot was the last person he needed in his life.

She walked out of the room, and he noticed that she held herself with enormous dignity. That was something he'd seen from the beginning with Sara.

The way she faced up to embarrassment, disappointment, and now, rejection. He thought of her in that meeting, how she'd held the division leaders in the palm of her hand.

So what the hell was he doing, thinking she could be part of the plant conspiracy? Where were his instincts, for God's sake? His razor-sharp intuition that had made him the best damn security officer in the Navy? She'd blocked his radar, jammed the controls. All with a look and a kiss.

A kiss. She'd broken him with that ridiculous kiss in the middle of a pond. He'd lost his mind back there, given in to some primitive urge that had no thought or care.

"They're not dry yet. They'll need another half hour, I think. If you'd like, I can give you a blanket to cover yourself, and drive you home. It won't be comfortable, but you'll be decent."

One look at her standing in the living room, her face clean and clear with no makeup to hide her vulnerability, and he lost his resolve. "No. I can wait."

She nodded once, then went into the kitchen to the refrigerator. She got a handful of ice and wrapped it in a towel, then she passed him without looking, and took a seat on the living-room couch.

She held the towel in her hands while she stared at the mantel above the fireplace. There were several pictures there, but he couldn't see the subjects from where he sat. He'd hurt her feelings. That much was clear.

Folding the robe tighter against him, feeling like a damn fool with the feathers and the silky, feminine material, he went to join her, even though he knew that it was a risky business. He didn't trust himself with her, especially when she had that look on her face.

They sat quietly for a few moments, he on one side of the couch, she on the other. The space between them wasn't much, yet it seemed an unbreachable chasm.

"Can I get you something to drink?" she asked.

"No, I'm fine. Thanks."

Another long silence filled the small room. He glanced at her, but she was looking at the mantel again. From here he could see the pictures. An older couple who might be her parents. Young girls in school uniforms. An old, old man, and two pictures of smiling nuns.

"Did you like it there?" he asked. "Your convent school?"

Sara followed his gaze to the picture of her teachers. "Very much. The nuns were smart and kind. They always treated me firmly, but fairly."

"Why Switzerland? Why not here in the States?"

She looked at him now, to find he had turned to face her. It was easy to dismiss the ludicrous robe, to see the man who wore it with the assurance of one who has nothing to prove. His face had lost its anger, an anger she didn't understand, but that she'd caused. "My father died before I was born. My mother, my grandmother and my aunt raised me, and they had all three gone to St. Mary's. I went there to carry on, I suppose."

"I hear your accent, but it's very slight."

She nodded. "We spoke English mostly. I do speak French and German, but I'm getting rusty."

"You came back here for college."

"Yes. I hadn't spent all that much time here, and I wanted to learn. I could have gone to a coed school, but I was frightened. I'd never been out on a date. I'd never even been around boys, except for the occasional dance at St. Vincent's. Those were always so awkward. I couldn't dance, and no one there could teach me, even though God knows, Sister Mary Francis tried. I grew up thinking boys were a different species altogether."

"We are."

She smiled. "Yes, I did get that right, after all, didn't I?"

"I've been around women my whole life. I started dating when I was fifteen. My dorm was coed. I listened in women's studies, and in beginning psyche. I even had a girlfriend for a long time, and I *know* we're separate species. More than that. We're from different planets."

"Men are from—"

"Mars. Right. So don't think you have the monopoly on confusion. If anything, you're probably smarter about this stuff than most. You don't have all that old baggage twisting things around."

"You don't have your girlfriend anymore?"

He shook his head. "Talk about baggage."

"That's not very nice."

"I don't mean it that way," he said, smiling at her indignant tone.

"Good. Because you must have loved her. I don't understand people who split apart and become such enemies. If you love someone, some part of that love has to stay."

"Sometimes there are reasons, Sara. Reasons why still loving that person would do nothing but harm. Sometimes, the bitterness is the only thing left that makes sense."

She shook her head. "I can't see it. You're a nice man. I can't imagine you with anyone but a nice girl. What reason could you have for being bitter? If it didn't work out between you, it's because you weren't a perfect match, that's all. You were meant for another. Simple."

"Simple?" Matt studied Sara's face. Her certainty. Breaking her heart would be a crime against humanity. He pitied the poor fool who fell in love with her. He'd be stuck for life, and then some. "It's not simple when the person you love betrays you."

"Betrayal. You mean she left you for someone else?"

How had he gotten himself into this conversation? He didn't want to talk about Kelly. It was private business, old business. "Yes, she did. But at least she had the courtesy to thank me for showing her that love was possible. And for introducing her to my best friend. It was all very civilized. We shook hands all around."

Sara's eyes changed, softening around the edges with pity. Matt stood up. "I've got to get going. I'll just change now. I can live with a little dampness."

"She wasn't the one, Matthew. But if you keep thinking she was, you won't be ready."

"Ready? For what?"

"Your true love."

He had to smile. "True love happens in fairy tales. And if you'll notice, all fairy tales end just after the wedding."

"I know many people who've been in love for years. Look at Juliet."

"Okay, I'll give you that. Sometimes it happens. But we're talking long shots here. The odds are astronomical."

She stood up, too. "The odds are so high because people have grown cynical. They've closed their hearts. Just like you. You don't believe it will happen, and you do whatever you have to, to be right."

"You think I don't want to find love? That I'm happy going home alone each night?"

"Yes, I do. I think you get out of life what you expect to get. You expect loneliness."

"You don't know me well enough to know what I expect."

"I see you at the office. You don't smile. You don't make friends. You suspect everyone and keep yourself separate. I may be naive, but I'm not stupid. I can see that the last thing you want in your life is love."

She took a step toward him and put her hand on his arm. He stared at her fingers on the pink material, the absurd color perfect somehow for this crazy conversation.

"It's not that simple," he said.

"That doesn't mean it's not true," she said, her voice just above a whisper.

He moved his arm and broke the contact. "Where's the dryer? I'll get the clothes."

She shook her head. "No. Wait here."

He watched her walk down the hall, shaken from the conversation, and upset that he was reacting at all. She was dangerous, all right. She had a way of creeping inside locked doors that were locked for a reason. He had no idea why he'd said so much. Or why he was letting her sophomoric ideas get to him. Taking love lessons from Sara was like learning about heavy artillery from Mr. Rogers. So why was he upset?

"They're pretty much dry," Sara said, as she came back down the hall.

He met her by the bathroom and took the folded sweats. "Thanks."

Sara smiled as graciously as she could as she gave him his clothes. He went to change, and she sighed.

She'd done everything wrong. Again. It didn't seem to matter that she wasn't trying to flirt. She just kept blowing it. It was a new phenomenon, something that had started when she'd accepted Juliet's challenge. The only logical thing to do was to stop. Cut her losses. Maybe she just wasn't ready for the man-woman thing to happen. She'd wait ten years, then try it again.

Her mistake was in taking the kiss seriously. He wasn't kissing *her* so much as he was kissing *someone*. She'd just been convenient. Because if he'd meant to kiss her, he wouldn't be leaving like this, would he? He'd find some reason to stick around. To get to know her better. To kiss her again.

She heard the bathroom door open, but she didn't turn to face him.

"I'll be going then," he said.

She pasted a smile on and headed for the front door. "Thanks again for helping with Sirius."

He walked slowly toward her, holding the robe across his arm. "Here," he said, handing it to her. "Thanks for the soup and all. It was really good."

"You're welcome."

He didn't move. She didn't move. The awkwardness in the room didn't move, either.

"Well," she said, grabbing the doorknob. She grimaced at the contact to her bruised hand.

"Hey," Matt said, taking that hand gently in his own. "You didn't put anything on this, did you?"

"I forgot."

He shook his head, and led her toward the bathroom. "It's gonna get infected if you don't take care of it. Now, what have you got in your medicine cabinet?" He swung the mirrored door open. Still holding on to her with one hand, he used the other to check the contents of her shelves. "Deodorant, powder, face cream, woman's thing, another woman's thing, hair spray, mouthwash, aspirin, woman's thing, aha."

He brought the spray antibiotic down, and turned her palm up. "This might hurt. You want a bullet to bite on?"

She laughed. "I can take it."

"Scream if you have to, Private. There's no shame in pain."

He sprayed her hand and it stung, but just for a second, and not very much. Or was it that she was preoccupied with his touch? Or the fact that he'd stuck around after all?

"Other hand."

She offered it up to him, and he ministered to her. It was a feeling she could get used to. His gaze intent, he clucked his tongue and shook his head over her very tiny wounds. She liked it when he had that worried crease in his forehead. It seemed sexy and masculine to her. His jaw competed for her attention, and won. The square, strong lines made her think of Greek gods, the good-looking ones. Or maybe Tyrone Power. He'd been her mother's favorite all these years, and Sara could see a slight resemblance. Although frankly, Matt was much better looking.

"I think you're going to make it," he pronounced. He put the spray back into the cupboard. "It's getting late. I'd better—"

"I didn't say thank you, did I?"

"Yeah."

"I meant for coming to the park. To tell me about Jim."

"Oh."

"So, uh, thanks for that."

"My pleasure. He would have come, but he had this thing."

"I'm sure. It was just nice of you to take the trouble is all."

"Well, I was going to be there anyway. For my run. I do that."

"It's good for you. But you look like you know that already."

"Yeah, I got used to a lot of physical fitness in the Navy."

"Right. The Navy. You were a sailor."

He smiled. "I was a SEAL, ma'am."

She nodded. "A SEAL."

"It means I was in a special corps. Trained for underwater actions."

"So you like to swim?"

"Couldn't you tell from this morning?"

She laughed, and it sounded loud in the small room. "I bet they're still wondering about that."

"Who?"

"The people at the park. We must have looked a sight."

"Well, the dog."

"Yes, he is something."

"You're not going to try that again, are you?"

"No, no. I've learned my lesson."

"I don't mean you shouldn't get a dog. Dogs can be great. It's just that he was so big."

"Right. If I get one, he'll be small."

"Well, not too small."

"No. Not too…"

Her words ran out as he moved his head that tiny distance between close and intimate. She moved with him. Waiting, anticipating. Knowing the kiss was coming. Breathless. His hypnotic gaze holding her captive.

His lips touched hers, and she was a goner.

# Chapter Eight

Matt pulled Sara close. He circled her with his arms, and used his mouth to tell her of his hunger. It had been so long since he'd felt like this, since he'd needed like this.

She was so soft and so willing. Her eager tongue touched his and he tasted all the sweetness in the world. He shouldn't be doing this, but he couldn't stop. Not for love nor money. She'd stolen his reason and replaced it with desire. When he felt her soft, pliant breasts against his chest, he was helpless to do anything but want her more.

He felt her hand on his chest, and it took a moment to realize she was pushing him back. She pulled away from his kiss, and he heard her say, "The doorbell."

Then he heard it, too. "Damn."

"I'd better—"

He nodded. When she left him, he felt like slamming his fist through the door. Not out of frustration, well, not *all* out of frustration, but out of anger at himself. What was wrong with him? Couldn't he control himself for five damn minutes?

"Jim!"

Matt left the bathroom and saw Forester at the front door. He was carrying flowers. It was a little late for that, wasn't it? *He* should have been in the park this morning, so that *he* could have gone swimming with the damn Great Dane. But then *he* would have kissed Sara, so—

"You're still here?"

Matt nodded. "That I am."

Jim smiled, then turned back to face Sara. "I came to apologize for not making our date," he said. "I thought these might help." He handed her the dozen pink roses.

"You didn't have to," Sara said, sniffing the bouquet. "But they're beautiful. I'll go put them in water. Please make yourself at home."

She left, and Matt crossed his arms. He didn't know what was up with Jim, and he wanted to find out. Just this morning, Forester had said he wasn't interested in Sara. That he didn't want to play spy anymore. That Matt was on his own. So why the about-face?

"I thought you'd be long gone by now."

Matt shook his head. "Still here."

"Had a good time at the park, did you?"

"It was just like you'd expect. Sara is a nice girl."

Jim went to the couch and sat down. He put his

arm on the backrest and crossed his legs, looking for all the world like he owned the place. Matt thought he looked stupid in his jogging suit. That shiny material was for old men and toddlers.

"You're right. She is a nice girl. Which is why I'm here." He looked up at Matt. "But I'll leave right now if you want me to. I mean, if something happened." He raised his brow, and Matt felt his anger climb from a dull heat to a full boil.

"Nothing happened. You can stay here all night if you want to. I don't care."

"Uh-huh." Jim nodded. "Then why are you standing there like the protector of the harem?"

Matt uncrossed his arms and walked over to the rocking chair. He sat down, and pushed himself back and forth, the chair's squeak keeping tempo. He looked at Jim. Jim looked back.

Finally Sara walked in from the kitchen with the vase of roses. She put them on the coffee table and looked from Jim to Matt and back again. "I didn't expect so much company today. Would either of you like a drink?"

"No, thanks," Matt said.

"Sure." Jim stood up. "Point me to the bar."

His smile to Sara was definitely friendly. Too friendly. What did he want? It wasn't the favor Matt had asked him for, to keep an eye on her in case she was involved in the corporate espionage. Had Jim suddenly realized just how attractive Sara was?

That thought stopped Matt for a moment. When

exactly had *he* realized how beautiful she was? He remembered meeting her for the first time. He'd sized her up quickly: sort of pretty, very shy, bookworm. She had a nice smile, but nothing to keep him up nights. So why had he been so intent on kissing her at the drop of a hormone? What had caused this incredible shift?

He looked at her now, standing on her toes to reach for a bottle in the cupboard. Dressed so simply in her T-shirt and jeans, he could see her figure was trim and firm, but then he'd realized that up close and personal. Her hair wasn't different, at least he didn't think so. Long, dark, shiny. She liked to braid it for work, but now it was loose around her shoulders. No, he just couldn't pinpoint a physical cause for her attractiveness. It had to be something deeper than that. Something he'd noticed when she'd poured her spaghetti onto his lap. But he couldn't name it. Maybe it had no name at all.

"Sure you don't want a drink?" Sara asked him as she came back to the living room. He smiled when he saw the liquor bottle was actually cooking sherry. Jim must just love that.

"No, thanks. I'm fine."

She ushered Jim to his seat on the couch, then she sat at the other end. Right between them. Only Jim's arm was closer to her.

Matt stretched his legs out, his foot only inches from her small bare feet. He smiled, then turned to his pal. "So you ended your date early, huh?"

"Date? I didn't have a date."

Matt nodded. "My mistake. I thought that's why you stood Sara up. Sorry."

"I didn't stand her up. I sent you. Remember?"

"Right. Right." He just kept rocking.

"I'm here now to make up for it." Jim turned to Sara. "I came to see if you'd come to dinner with me tonight. To make up for this morning."

Sara looked quickly at Matt, then back to Jim. "Oh, I don't know…"

"It's the least I can do. I stuck you with this big lug, after all. I owe you for that."

"Big lug?" Matt said, leaning forward.

Jim laughed. "Can't take a joke there, Quartermain? What's happened to your famous sense of humor?"

Matt almost said what he wanted to, but Sara spoke first.

"I know," Sara said, a little too loudly. But it worked, because it brought Jim's attention back to her. "We'll all three go. Isn't that right, Matt?"

She turned to him with pleading eyes. "You can go home and change. I need to shower. It'll be fun. We're a team, aren't we?"

Matt studied her for a long minute. He tried to think of something worse than sitting in a restaurant, watching Sara and Jim flirt with each other, but he couldn't. On the other hand, he didn't trust his buddy as far as he could throw him. But Sara— She might get herself into a situation she couldn't handle. "You bet. We'll all change and meet back here at what, seven?"

Jim gave him the look of death. "Great. I'm so glad you're tagging along, Matt, old friend."

"My pleasure."

"I believe it."

"We got dragged into the pond."

Matt and Jim both looked at Sara, and she smiled, trying to look casual and perky at the same time.

"What?" Jim took a sip of his drink and grimaced.

"Matt and I. We were walking Sirius, and the leash got tangled, and we went into the lake. We couldn't move an inch. Everyone was pointing and laughing. Finally the man came and got Sirius so he could get his duck. It was really quite exciting."

Jim stared at Sara, then his drink, then back to Sara. "What?"

"She told you just like it was, my man. A regular play-by-play. But I guess you had to be there. Right, Sara?"

Sara nodded. "I guess."

Matt stood up. "We'd better let the lady get a little rest before the big dinner tonight, eh?"

Jim shook his head, then stood up, too. "Right." He turned to Sara again. "The man got his duck?"

"No, Sirius got his duck. Well, not really, but he came close."

There was a very long pause. Matt was having a hell of a time keeping a straight face.

"Seven o'clock. Here. Right?"

Sara walked them both to the door. "I'll be ready. Thank you for the flowers, Jim."

She squeezed Matt's hand just as he stepped outside. "Thank you for, well, for everything."

Matt gave Jim a glance, then took Sara's hand in his. He kissed it gently. "You're a real surprise."

Sara stared at both men. She didn't know what to do or say. Or how to get the butterflies in her stomach to stop fluttering. So instead of speaking, or taking even a tiny chance at blowing this once in a lifetime, earthshaking, monumental moment in her male-deprived life, she closed the door.

She hugged herself tightly a second later. Two men. Beautiful men. Fighting over *her!* Well, not fighting. But both of them wanted her attention. That was for real. Juliet would be thrilled. She'd been right all along. All Sara had to do was follow the lessons in the book. Take them one by one, and voilà! She was the belle of the ball, the princess at the prom.

It was too delicious to let go. She wanted to think about what Matt had said, how Jim had looked, how Matt had kissed her. Kissed her very breath away.

She hurried to the bathroom and drew herself a bath. She even took the perfumed beads she'd gotten for her last birthday and sprinkled them liberally in the water. She had time for a nice long soak, and a replay of every last detail of that kiss.

IT WAS MATT who ended up taking her to the emergency room. Jim offered, but Matt insisted.

He'd been so nice about it, too. He didn't ask her why she'd told the waiter she'd have what Jim was having, without even checking to see if the dish had shellfish. Which was a good thing, because she never would have admitted that it was simply step ten. He hadn't even asked her why she'd kept laughing at Jim's somewhat pedestrian jokes after the hives had popped out all over her face and hands. She'd have been too humiliated to admit that she was just following orders, number eleven to be exact. And he'd never even questioned why she'd spent so much time paying attention to Jim, and not him.

That would have required the hardest explanation of all. How in the world could she tell Matt that she'd been afraid to stop flirting with Jim because she didn't want Matt to lose interest in her?

She'd figured the whole thing out in the bathtub. Matt and Jim were vying for her attention. On that count, she was certain. But would they be vying for that attention if they didn't each think the other man was going to win?

No one had paid this kind of attention to her at the company ever. Now, two men—two very charming, successful, beautiful men—were showing up with roses and tea...

Matt had surprised her with that one. When he'd come to pick her up for dinner, he'd brought a tin of exotic teas. He'd noticed her English pot and cozy and the lovely cups and saucers she'd brought back from Europe. He'd noticed, and had brought her something for *her*.

But by then she'd figured out the reason he was being so attentive. Competition. They were both trying so hard, in their own ways, to make her smile, to let her feel special. It had to be some sort of male thing, something that Juliet would have to explain to her.

In the meantime, all she'd been able to do was follow the instructions in Flirting 101. So far, despite her clumsiness, everything Juliet had suggested had worked. And if she'd bothered to make her own selection at dinner, it would still be working.

Instead she was sitting in an examining room, trying very hard not to scratch, while Matt was stuck in the waiting room, next to triplets with croup and a man with a bowling ball stuck to his hand.

If only life had a rewind button, she thought. She'd go back and order soup. No. If she could turn back time, she'd go back farther—right to the moment Matt had kissed her.

She scratched her chin, and shook her head as she looked at her arms and legs. Big red blotches covered her skin. The nice young doctor had gone to get her some medication for the swelling and itching, but it would take a long while for the welts to go away.

"Hey, you doing okay?"

Matt stood in the doorway, a concerned frown making his brow furrow.

"I'll be fine. I just have to wait to get some pills. It's not life-threatening or anything like that."

"Good," he said, walking all the way inside the small room. "You scared me there for a minute."

"It's my own fault. I should have checked what I was eating."

"We all make mistakes."

"I've used up my quota for the year, don't you think?"

He smiled, and she felt instantly better. "I think you need a keeper, is what I think, Ms. Cabot. Someone to watch over you."

"Normally I don't, though. I'm really a very capable person. Ask anyone. I can dress myself, and drive a car, and they even let me vote. It's only around you—" She stopped, startled at the realization that her mishaps really did seem to all be connected to Matt. Not Jim. Matt.

"I can leave, if that will make you feel safer," he said.

She shook her head. "Oh, no. Don't do that. I'm glad you're here."

He moved closer to her, his gaze steady and clear. "Are you?"

She nodded. "But I think, maybe I'm allergic to you. Like shellfish. Only with you, I break out in mistakes."

He lifted her hand and very gently rubbed the

tender, swollen skin. "You haven't done anything wrong," he said. "Nothing permanent, at least. Nothing that matters." He narrowed his eyes a bit. "Have you?"

"Well, no one's died. Yet."

He started to say something, then stopped. But when she didn't fill in the silence, he finally spoke. "I don't want to see you get hurt, Sara."

"Hey, I've got insurance."

"Not for the kind of hurt I'm talking about."

She looked at him for a long time, her hives forgotten, the world forgotten. "Oh, I see."

"Do you?"

"I think so."

He took her other hand in his, careful not to put any pressure on them. "The thing is, I like you. I really do. That's why I have to warn you."

She held her breath.

"You be careful about Jim, okay? He's... He's a nice guy, but he's a little sophisticated for you. He might want to go a little too fast."

Jim? He was warning her about Jim?

The knock on the door startled her and she looked up to see Dr. Mallery walk in.

"Here we go," he said, handing her two pills and a paper cup with water. "Take these now, and I'll give you a course to take at home. I'm also giving you a prescription for some bath powder that should help. And next time, stay away from that shrimp."

She put the pills into her mouth, but it was hard

to swallow, even with the water. She wanted to ask Matt what he meant. If his warning was just friend to friend, or if he was trying to get Jim out of the picture. She couldn't believe the hope that swelled inside her. How could she have been so silly? After that kiss, those two kisses, she'd known. She'd known with a certainty that was as bright as the lights above her. She didn't want Jim Forester. She never had. It was Matt she wanted. In the few short days she'd been around him, he'd grabbed on to her heart. She looked at him now, capturing his gaze, trying to read the meaning deep inside.

"Any other questions?" Dr. Mallery asked.

She nodded, still holding Matt's gaze steady. "What about…you?"

He looked away, and in that one second she realized he didn't want her the way she wanted him. Despite the kisses. The kisses that had seemed like love to her, but must have been sport to him.

"I shouldn't have kissed you today," Matt said.

Sara vaguely heard the doctor clear his throat, then leave. All her concentration was on the man in front of her.

"No, you shouldn't have."

"I didn't intend to."

"I see."

"No, that's not what I meant." He let her hands go, and walked to the side of the tiny room. He absently picked up a box of gloves, then put them down again, and turned to her. "I had no business kissing you today. Not that I didn't like it. I did. That's the problem. I can't get involved with you, Sara. Not right now.''

"I don't recall asking you to.''

He had the good manners to blush. "I know. It's my fault, not yours. I took advantage, and I'm sorry about that. But I'm not sorry about getting to know you. I hope you can believe that.''

She nodded, and slid down off the examination table. "Of course I can. I'm a very nice person. Naive, sweet and nice. I'm also very tired, and if you don't mind, I'd like to go home.''

"Wait a minute.''

"Why?''

"Because this isn't turning out right.''

"I'm used to that, Mr. Quartermain. Don't worry about it.''

He touched her chin and brought her gaze up to meet his. "I think you are sweet and nice, and not nearly as naive as I thought you were.''

"Oh, but I am. Or maybe naive isn't the word. Maybe I'm just plain foolish.''

"I GIVE UP,'' Sara said. "It's all fallen apart, and I can't make it right again.''

"But, *chérie*,'' Juliet said, handing her a tissue. "Everything is perfect.''

"Weren't you listening? Didn't you hear what he said to me?''

Juliet nodded. "I heard every word, Sara. And more. I heard what he meant."

"Oh, no. I don't even want to go there. You're the dangerous one. Not me."

"Did you or did you not get soundly kissed yesterday?"

Sara nodded, glad the door to the office was closed so no passerby would hear this conversation.

"Did you or did you not have two men squabble over you?"

She nodded once more.

"And did you or did you not feel your heart come to life?"

Sara reluctantly nodded again. "Immediately followed by its quick and untimely death."

"Your heart is anything but dead, *chérie*. It's very much alive, and if you listen carefully, it will tell you what you must do."

"I assume you can hear it from all the way over there, right?"

Juliet smiled. The phone rang, and while Juliet spoke about business, Sara tried to listen to her heart. What should she do? Give up? Join the convent? Find a hobby that would comfort her in her old age, like knitting or stamp collecting?

"What you must do is finish the course," Juliet said as soon as she was off the phone. "Only now, you must change your focus."

"To whom?"

"Matthew, of course."

Sara couldn't believe her ears. "Are you crazy? He told me in no uncertain terms he wasn't interested in me."

"That's what he said. Not what he meant."

"So he was lying?"

"Not exactly lying. It was more that he didn't know the truth himself."

"And that truth is—?"

"He's already half in love with you, Sara."

"Right. The bottom half."

Juliet laughed. "You listen to me. I'm not wrong about this. Today you will go to his office. Find out what he likes, what he doesn't like. Mirror his movements when you see him next. Touch his arm. Pay attention to him. Just follow the steps, darling. Follow the steps. Love is waiting at the end of the road."

# Chapter Nine

Sara checked the hallway in front of Matt's office, and when she was sure no one was around, she opened his door. Feeling too much like a double agent, she closed the door behind her and flattened herself against the wall. She could feel her heart pounding in her chest. It wasn't just that she was sneaking into his office, but that she was sneaking into *his* office.

Her first impression was that the room didn't fit him. It was the same size as Jim's, had the same general decor, only Matt's color scheme consisted of mostly browns and leather, and there were no dolls on the shelves.

There was nothing personal that she could see from where she stood. No pictures. No mementos. Nothing that made her feel his presence. She moved over to his desk.

It wasn't as obsessively neat as Jim's, and that was something of a relief. The papers were of no interest to her, except for the fact that it reminded her of step twenty-five. She turned to the small trash bin under his desk and picked out a piece of paper he'd written on. It didn't matter what it said, just that it had his handwriting.

That was another of Juliet's skills—handwriting analysis. Sara stuffed the note into her purse, then looked once more at the desk.

She touched the back of his chair and the smooth, cool leather gave her the first real sense that Matt worked here. Knowing it was foolish, knowing he could walk in any minute, she sat down. It was almost like sitting in his lap. She could *feel* him in the soft cushioned seat, smell his scent faintly when she turned her head. But there was no more time left for that. She had to learn what she could and leave before anyone was the wiser.

Moving quickly, she got up, went to the wall with the shelves and looked at the books there. All business, nothing personal. Darn it. She wasn't getting anything she could use. And there was no more time to look. She headed for the door, and nearly leapt out of her skin when it opened.

She jumped back, her pulse racing, her face hot, and tried to remember the excuse she'd written down before leaving her own office. Only it wasn't Matt who walked in. It was Jim. And he was smiling, as if finding her here in Matt's office was what he'd expected.

"All the hives are gone," he said casually. "I'm glad."

She nodded. "The medicine works quickly."

"I'm just sorry it broke up our dinner last night."

"Yes," she said, moving slowly toward the door. "I'm sorry, too."

Jim went over to Matt's desk, and put his briefcase down, so at-ease and comfortable she started to feel foolish for her own sense of drama. "So where'd the big guy go?" Jim asked.

"I'm not sure. I thought he would be back by now."

Jim nodded. "Well, I'm glad he's not here. I don't need the competition."

She laughed nervously. "Competition?"

He snapped open his briefcase and took out a silver-wrapped package. He turned to her, his gaze sliding down her body, his smile just sexy enough to make her nervous.

"It's lucky I found you here, though. I've got a little present for you."

"Oh?"

He handed her the box. "Go ahead. Open it."

She continued staring at him for a moment, not happy at all that they were still in Matt's office, where she didn't belong. Not even happy to get a present, despite the fact that presents were something she normally loved. She tore the pretty paper, and uncovered a bottle of perfume. Obsession.

"Oh, this is...very lovely," she said.

Jim came close, and slipped the beautiful oval bottle from her hand. He lifted the cap off, and leaned in, very close. He moved her hair back behind her ear and sprayed the perfume lightly on her skin. "You still owe me a dinner, Sara," he whispered.

"But we had dinner last night."

He shook his head as he moved the bottle behind her other ear. "That wasn't what I had in mind. I want it to be just you and me. So we can talk. I want to get to know you better."

He leaned that final inch until his lips touched hers. It was a brief kiss, a peck actually. Then he caught her gaze in his. "A lot better," he said. Then he kissed her for real.

"What the hell?"

Sara pushed Jim away with all her strength. He stumbled back into the bookcase, and for a moment, she thought all the books were going to tumble down on him. They shook but didn't fall, so she turned to face Matt standing in the doorway.

"Hi," she said.

"Hello."

"Um, that wasn't... I didn't... He, uh..."

"I see."

"No, that's not it at all!"

"Sorry about using your office, buddy," Jim said.

His voice held no guilt, no remorse. Sara thought it might even be a little cocky, which wasn't fair. "I was looking for you," she said, imploring Matt to believe her.

"We just got a little carried away," Jim said. He

walked over to her and put one arm around her waist and handed her the perfume with the other. "We shouldn't have done that. Right, Sara?"

She sidestepped out of his embrace, wondering what in the heck she'd done so wrong. Okay, so she'd snuck into Matt's office. That was a bad thing. But Juliet had assured her that all was fair in love and war, and that it wasn't as if she was snooping for a wicked reason. Besides, the last thing she'd wanted was for Jim to show up, or to kiss her like that. She'd changed her focus, for goodness' sake. Couldn't Jim tell?"

"I have to go," she said, as she eased her way toward the door.

Matt's face seemed set in stone, disapproval coming off him in waves. She wanted to tell him what had really happened, but that was impossible. Only how could she leave him with the impression that she'd actively participated in that kiss?

"He surprised me," she said.

Jim cleared his throat. "She's right. I was out of line. I apologize, Sara. I must have misunderstood. I have no excuse for kissing you here, anyway. You both have my apology."

She looked from Matt to Jim and back again. Matt was still angry, although she wasn't quite sure if it was finding her in his office without permission or finding her kissing Jim that was the real culprit. Then she remembered what Matt had said last night. How he didn't want to get involved with her. That cleared up the question of why he was angry. He wanted her to leave him alone.

As for Jim, she had to acknowledge that she was just as much to blame for the kiss as he was. She'd used over half her steps on him already. He'd simply responded, just as Juliet had predicted. Just as she'd wanted him to, a couple of days ago. She wasn't entirely sure what a petard was, but she felt pretty certain that she'd just been hoisted by her own.

Both men were looking at her. Waiting for her to say something. In the world of awkward pauses, this was a gold medal moment, one she'd surely be reliving in nightmares for a long time to come. She opened her mouth, but no words came out. She tried to smile, but that didn't work, either. All she could do was turn on her heel and walk out the door.

Matt watched her leave, still more upset than he cared to be. It wasn't that the two of them were in his office without permission. It was that damn kiss. He turned slowly to Jim, wanting very much to wipe that smile off his face with his fist.

"She was at it again," Jim said.

"What?"

"Snooping. I found her looking through your desk."

"So, you figured you'd kiss the truth out of her?"

"Hey, you were the one who asked me to get close to her."

"I didn't mean in the biblical sense."

"No? Well, it seems like a mighty fine way to me."

Matt unclenched his fists and went behind his desk. "Is that why you're here? Or did you have some other business?"

Jim smiled at him. "What's gotten into you? Are you jealous?"

Matt sat down. "No. I am not jealous."

"Yes, you are. Your face is all red. You're angry about that kiss, aren't you? Just what exactly happened Saturday morning, huh? Did you two—?"

"No."

"But you wanted to, right?"

Matt silently counted to five. "Listen, Forester. For the record, I don't believe Sara is involved with the thefts. I'll still keep an eye on her, strictly for the sake of the case, but I'd stake my reputation that she's completely innocent."

"Even though I found her going through your papers?"

He nodded. "I'm sure she had a logical reason for doing that. Which I intend to discover."

Jim nodded. "Fine. So you're not interested in her personally, right?"

Matt shook his head. "No."

"Good," Jim said, closing his briefcase. "Because I am. For what it's worth, I agree with you. I don't think she's involved. At least not intentionally. She's too nice a kid to steal from the company." He walked to the door, and just before he left he turned once more to Matt. "But just to be on the safe side, I'm going to keep a close eye on her. If it turns into something more, I won't complain." He winked, then walked away.

Matt yanked open his top drawer and plucked the tennis ball from the back corner. He squeezed it so hard he thought it might break.

Sitting became impossible. He stood up, banging his knee on the opened drawer, and cussed until he ran out of words. How dare that arrogant bastard kiss Sara? How dare he kiss her *here*. How come she was in here, anyway? What the hell was she doing going through his papers? And what the hell was she doing to his brains?

He studied his desk. Everything looked as if it was in place. If she had gone through his papers, she'd been damn neat about it. What he'd said to Jim was the truth. He didn't believe Sara was capable of stealing from the company. So why had she looked through his things?

And why had she kissed Jim? Only two days ago, she'd been in his arms. Kissing him as if she meant it. Or maybe he just wanted to believe that. Hadn't she been paying Jim a lot of attention? Hadn't he known she was going after Forester, and not him?

He squeezed the ball again. This was nuts. He was totally out of control here, and for what? He didn't have any interest in Sara Cabot. He couldn't have. She was too young, too naive. She needed too much. Let Jim be the one to teach her. Let him give her everything and watch her walk away. Let him get his heart trampled when she said goodbye.

"Fine," he said aloud. "Good riddance."

But it wasn't fine. Dammit. It wasn't fine at all. He took a deep, calming breath, then he sneezed, hard, five times in a row.

WHEN SARA SAW MATT standing at the door to her office, her first instinct was to crawl under her desk. She held back, somehow, and even managed a smile. "Come on in."

He did, and she could already tell this wasn't going to be a pleasant visit. He still had that angry look in his eyes.

"I'm sorry about before," she said. "I shouldn't have been in your office."

He nodded a polite greeting to Juliet, then took a seat across from Sara. "So why were you?"

She blinked. She hadn't expected him to ask her that, at least not so abruptly. But she'd prepared. She'd written down the excuse before she'd gone to his office. So why was her mind a total blank?

The seconds ticked by, and she could see his impatience swell.

"Sara was waiting to ask you about some security measures," Juliet said.

Sara looked at her, grateful beyond words. "Yes. Security measures. That's right."

"What kind of security measures?"

Her gaze went back to Matt. Unfortunately, her thought process didn't engage.

"She wanted to know if she should take her computer disks home, or leave them in the office. Isn't that right, Sara?"

She looked at Juliet once again, and nodded. "Home," she repeated. "Or office."

"I see," Matt said. But he didn't buy it. His eyes were scrunched and that was a sure sign of disbelief. Then they scrunched some more, and his whole face scrunched with it. He sneezed, loudly.

"God bless you."

"Uh-huh. So you came to my...to my..." He sneezed again, covering his mouth with his hand.

"God bless you."

He nodded, but she could tell he was getting ready to sneeze some more. She reached for a tissue and handed it to him, and he proceeded to use it four, five times.

"Are you okay?"

"Allergic to something," he said. He stood up, backing away from her as if she was a carrier. "We'll discuss..." He didn't get the words out. He just sneezed over and over again as he left the office. She heard him all the way down the hall. He was allergic all right. To her.

"That was lucky," Juliet said.

"Lucky? The poor man was in pain."

"It was lucky he didn't stay here to question you.

He probably thinks you're the one stealing the company secrets.''

Sara didn't find that funny at all. ''Do you think so?''

Juliet shook her head. ''He's more sensible than that. But you must have more confidence in yourself, *chérie*. Remember step twenty-seven.

Sara nodded. ''You're right. It was just that kiss…''

''That kiss should build your confidence higher than ever. It's working, don't you see?''

''Yes, but it's working on the wrong man.''

''No, it's working on both men.''

Sara stared hard at her friend. ''I'm not that good, Juliet.''

''My techniques are.''

''So tell me, teacher. What am I supposed to do about Jim?''

''Do?''

''Yes.''

Juliet leaned back in her chair and closed her eyes. As always, Sara was amazed at the quiet beauty of the woman. Despite her years, there were almost no lines in her face. Her silver hair made her look something like an angel. Only Sara knew that she was far more devil than cherub.

''He asked you out again, didn't he?''

Sara nodded.

''So, go out with him.''

''What?''

"Go out with him. But let Matt know you're going out with him."

For the first time since this adventure had begun, Sara felt the need to put her foot down. "No. I won't do that."

"Why not?"

"Because I don't want anyone to get hurt."

"Anyone? Or Matthew?"

"Anyone." She stood up and went over to Juliet's desk. "I don't want to play them against each other. It's not nice, and it's not fair."

"Nothing in love is fair, Sara."

"Well, it should be. It's enough that I'm using your wizard's tricks."

Juliet nodded. "You're right. It wouldn't be fair. They would probably end up killing each other."

"God forbid."

Juliet laughed. "That's the trouble with you Americans. You're so squeamish."

"And you call us barbarians," Sara said.

"So what are you going to do now?"

"Step twenty-seven."

"Good girl."

THE ANTIHISTAMINE kicked in a half hour later, and Matt was unbelievably grateful. He hadn't had an attack like that in years. Not since he'd been a kid and had stumbled into a field of buttercups. He looked at himself in the bathroom mirror, and wiped his nose again. His eyes were as red as stoplights.

He should have picked up some Visine while he was at the pharmacy.

None of which had anything to do with the fact that he still didn't know why Sara had been in his office. He didn't believe Juliet's excuse. It was logical, but not right. Something was fishy there, and he had to find out what. It was still possible that Sara was being blackmailed. Although, if that were the case, he wished she'd come to him.

Sniffing one last time, he left the rest room, but stopped short in front of the ladies' room door. Sara was in there. Talking to someone. Loudly.

He looked down the hall to make sure he was alone, then moved closer to the door to listen. Yes, it was Sara, all right. And now she was laughing.

"Stop it," she said. "You're making me blush."

Was Jim in there with her? That was crazy. Even Jim would know better than to go into the ladies' rest room in the middle of the day.

"We can never be together," she said, her voice dripping with passion. "The two of us, we're not right for each other. You know that. I know that. It will only bring us pain."

That's it. Jim was in there, all right. And he wasn't taking no for an answer.

"All right, darling. Just one kiss. Then we must part."

Matt squared his shoulders and pushed his way into the ladies' room. Sara's scream scared the hell out of him, but only for a second. "Where is he?"

"Who?"

"You know who." He looked behind the door, then into each cubicle. The man had disappeared. "Where is he?"

"Who?"

"Jim?"

"What?

"You were just talking to him."

"No, I wasn't."

"I heard you!" He focused on her, trying to will the truth out of her. But she just stood there, looking flustered and as beautiful as all get-out, a paperback book in one hand, her purse in the other.

"I was just reading."

"Reading?"

She held up the book. He couldn't see the title, but the cover told him it was a romance novel. "Reading?"

She nodded. "I do that sometimes."

"Out loud? In the bathroom?"

She cleared her throat. "The acoustics are good in here."

"Acoustics."

"You keep repeating what I say."

"I do," he said, more confused than a man ought to be. "I do."

Just then the door swung open and Lilly Marsh walked inside. She stopped suddenly, gasping when she saw Matt.

Matt nodded, trying his best to look as if he was

in there for a logical reason. "Excuse me," he said. "I'll just be leaving now."

He walked past his boss's wife, past Sara with her read-aloud book and out the door. And the first thing he did was sneeze.

# Chapter Ten

The missing disk was discovered just after lunch. Matt's beeper went off with a single message: Report to Marsh. He hurried to the elevator and went up to the top floor of the building. Marsh's office covered half the floor, and his secretary looked grim as he passed her on his way to the inner sanctum.

"It's got to stop," Ralph Marsh said without preamble. "You've got to stop it."

Matt nodded. "Which one was taken?"

"Sir Quack-A-Lot."

"Damn."

"That's an understatement. Get him, Matt. I need this finished."

"I've got a few ideas about what's going on. I can't tell you yet, but I'm pretty certain."

"When?" Marsh, a big man with a full head of toupee rose from his executive chair. He walked around the biggest desk Matt had ever seen and stood underneath his portrait. Matt knew it was his portrait because his name was etched in gold script on the bottom, but it didn't look anything like Marsh. The man in the portrait was fifteen years younger, fifty pounds thinner and smiling.

"Soon."

"That's not good enough, Matt. Soon won't make any of the stockholders happy."

"I can't give you anything more specific, Ralph. But I won't let you down."

Marsh studied him critically, his brows coming to an unsettling V. "I know you won't," he said, finally. "Do what you have to. Just do it fast."

Matt nodded, then left the big man's office. He stopped by Karen's desk, and the executive secretary smiled sympathetically. "That must have been fun."

Matt chuckled. "A barrel of laughs. Listen, I'm going to need some personnel files. Strictly confidential. You and me only, okay?"

She nodded. "I can do that."

"Good," he said. Then he proceeded to give her a very short list of names.

SARA LEFT THE OFFICE twenty minutes early. It's not that she had to punch a time clock or even had set hours, but in all the time she'd worked at Willard and Marsh, she'd made it a point to stay till six. It wasn't a hardship—she loved her job. She loved the kids, the ideas, the freedom she had to be creative. But right now, she had to get the heck out.

Things were getting too complicated. This whole flirting scheme had turned her life upside-down, and it was happening so fast! Juliet was certain everything was going to turn out perfectly, but Sara figured she had to say that—it was her plan. Sara felt no such thing.

A knot had settled in her stomach just after Matt had caught her doing her practice conversations in the ladies' room, and it hadn't gone away. She'd even had chamomile tea, which usually did the trick. But her poor brew was no match for the aftereffects of Matt Quartermain.

The man thought she was completely insane, and she couldn't blame him. He'd even started having psychosomatic allergies to her, sneezing whenever she was near. Now, how was she supposed to get him to kiss her again, with all that to contend with?

And then, of course, the entire Jim situation was completely out of control. After this morning's fiasco in Matt's office, Jim had sent her flowers of apology with a lovely, sincere note.

She had to face the fact that Jim's attentions were all her fault. She'd invited him to kiss her. Nearly asked him straight to his face. So how could she complain when he followed through?

Sister Mary Claire had told her many times to be careful what she wished for, that she might get it. At the time, Sara had thought the expression quaint but somewhat dim. Now she should probably make a sampler of the quote and hang it above her bed.

She didn't want Jim. She did want Matt. She could have Jim. Matt thought she was a fruitcake.

She looked up toward the heavens. "Very amusing. Now stop it."

She got into her Toyota, but didn't start the car immediately. The truth was, she didn't know where to go. Home was out of the question. She felt sure that all she would do there was picture Matt as he'd been on Saturday. Sitting on the couch. At the dining-room table in her silly pink robe. Stretching his legs out so they almost touched her feet. Standing in her bathroom the second before he'd kissed her.

No. Home was not the place to be. The park also had too many associations with Matt and her problem. Finally she decided to go to the movies. She drove toward the multiplex, hoping fervently that the Jane Austen film was still there. A good dose of Regency manners and misunderstandings was just what the doctor ordered.

MATT WAITED until every last person had gone and the building was locked before he went into Sara's office. He didn't like doing this, but he had no choice. He had to make sure she was in the clear. Although an investigation of her office wouldn't completely eliminate her as a suspect, it was the first step in doing just that.

He turned on the light and gave the office a quick once-over, concentrating on Sara's desk and her shelves. He'd never realized before how cozy she'd made the place, for an office at least. It wasn't just the dolls lining the shelves—almost everyone in the company had those. It was the knickknacks, the pictures of her family, the fresh flowers, the teapot on the back shelf. The room felt like Sara, and the farther he went inside, the more relaxed he felt.

He did a quick survey of the shelves and found nothing of interest there. Then it was on to Juliet's desk, but again, nothing. It wasn't until he was seated at Sara's desk, in her chair, which was way too low to the ground for his comfort, that he saw something that made him pause. It was a notebook, almost hidden beneath this month's production logs. He pulled the book out and opened the cover.

What he saw inside stopped him cold. He read it from word one to the last page. Then he read it again.

It was a flirting manual. Step by step seduction. A battle plan so well thought-out that the intended victim had no chance of escape. It was Machiavellian in its complexity, diabolical in its intent. But worst of all, it was all about Jim Forester.

He sneezed, seven times in a row.

SHE ENDED UP SEEING the new Jim Carrey movie. It was a far cry from Jane Austen, but it did keep her mind occupied. She even managed one or two laughs, although most of the film was entirely too juvenile for her taste. Unfortunately her problems were waiting for her right outside the theater door.

There were simply no more excuses. She had to go home. She took the scenic route, which meant she passed the park instead of going on the freeway. Seeing the pond made her all weepy, which in turn made her angry. Furious.

Why was she feeling like this? It was an experiment, that's all. These were practice men, for heaven's sake. There wasn't going to be a happy ending, at least not the kind of happy ending *she'd* choose if she were in charge.

Juliet had promised her that Jim would notice her. That she'd find out what it was like to flirt, and to have a man flirt back. The guarantee said nothing about happily ever after. She'd added that without Juliet's help.

Whatever agony she was going through now was her own darn fault. There was no one to blame but herself, and she'd better get used to that.

And she'd better stop thinking about that happily ever after part right here and now. Because if she didn't, she was going to be one very miserable flirting expert.

So why was it that the second she walked in her door, she pictured Matt on the couch? That she couldn't get him out of her mind as she changed clothes, or made herself some tea, or brushed her teeth? And why was it that he was the last thing she thought about before she fell asleep, and the first thing she thought about when she woke up?

IT WAS CLEAR she should have eaten lunch in her office. She should have made herself a sandwich, with some carrot sticks and an apple. It would have been a very nice lunch. And she wouldn't be sitting between Jim Forester and Matt Quartermain, as she was now.

"So," Matt said, smiling way too brightly to be earnest. "How are you two kids today?" He flipped open his napkin so violently, she felt sure he was going to knock his soda off the table.

"I'm all right," she said, trying to figure out why that smile made her want to dive for cover. "How are you?"

"Just peachy," he said, then turned to Jim. "How's tricks, Jim old boy? Keeping yourself out of trouble?"

Jim didn't meet Matt's eyes. Sara understood. Matt's eyes seemed quite daunting this afternoon. Almost, well, crazy.

"I'm good, Matt, thank you for asking. Spent some time with Ralph and Lilly last night. Lovely couple. They talked about you."

"Oh?" Matt said, stabbing a piece of potato as if he meant to kill it.

"Yep, they just can't say enough about you, kiddo. It was Matt this and Matt that. It was impossible to get a word in edgewise."

"I'll bet you managed."

Sara started planning her escape. She thought about grabbing her throat, pretending to choke and running from the room. But with her luck, both Matt and Jim would chase after her and fight over who got to do the Heimlich maneuver. Scratch Plan A. If only she'd had the foresight to order spaghetti. Then she'd know just what to do.

"It's a darn shame you haven't had any luck with your investigation there, Matt." Jim shook his head. "Tough break."

"Yes, well, you never know."

Jim's right brow raised. "Something new?"

Matt concentrated on his meal. "Maybe."

"Oh, a mystery. How about that, Sara. He's got something and he won't tell us."

"I don't want to know," she said. "It's upsetting to think that someone we all work with is doing these horrible things."

"You have any guesses?" Jim asked her.

She shook her head. "No. I don't even like to think about it."

Jim nodded. "I have something for you to think about. I've got tickets to the Arena for Friday night. Tony Bennett. Will you come?"

"No," Matt said, jumping in before she could open her mouth.

"What?" Jim asked.

"No, she's busy Friday."

"Really?"

Sara watched the two men volley, her gaze going from one to the other as if she were watching a tennis match. What she didn't understand was why she wasn't a part of this conversation. It was her they were talking about, wasn't it? And what was Matthew up to anyway?

"When did you ask her out?" Jim asked. He sounded very suspicious.

"Who said I asked her out?"

"Then how do you know she's busy?"

"I just do."

"Telepathy?"

"Yeah. That's right. ESP."

"So what's she doing if she's not going out with you?"

"That's for her to say."

"Yeah?"

"Yeah."

Then both men turned to glare at her, the source of all their troubles.

"I've got a perfect solution," she said. "You two can go out on the date together. I've got a headache, and it's not going away until Saturday." She stood up, angry, confused, but completely sure that she needed to get away.

Jim stood up so quickly that he lost his balance and bumped into her. Her purse fell to the ground, spilling its contents on the linoleum floor. Lipstick, hairbrush, car keys, pack of tissues, and a floppy disk. A floppy disk that wasn't hers.

Matt stood slowly. She looked at him, but his gaze was squarely on the disk. He bent to her purse and put everything back in. Everything except the disk. He looked at it, then turned to look up at her. "Where'd you get this?"

She shook her head. "It's not mine. I don't know where it came from."

Matt studied Sara's face. If she was lying, she was damn good. She seemed genuinely surprised. Confused. Innocent. But then he remembered the flirting book. Sara wasn't quite the innocent he'd once believed. She was far more devious than he'd given her credit for. Her plan to catch Jim was detailed and diabolical. What man could resist a plan like that?

He stood, keeping hold of the disk with the plans for Sir Quack-A-Lot. His instincts told him that the discovery was too convenient to be anything but a setup. But then, his instincts had been wrong many times when it came to Sara.

"Who do you think planted it there?" Jim said.

Matt's gaze went to Forester. Was it possible the two of them were in this scheme together? That the flirting book was just a ruse to disguise a crime spree? That made no sense.

Although nothing would give him greater pleasure than pinning this whole thing on Jim, the facts didn't add up. Jim was a large shareholder in Willard and Marsh, and every time a plan was stolen it was in effect taking money right out of Jim's pocket. Jim might be annoying, but he wasn't stupid. While Matt didn't completely eliminate him as a suspect, he hadn't found a thing that would indicate Jim's complicity.

Sara, on the other hand, had plenty of motive. But that didn't seem to matter. Matt knew she was innocent, dammit. Even after finding the book. He'd never been more certain about anything in his life. Sara was being set up. Now the question was, by whom?

"You do believe me," she asked, first him, then Jim. "Don't you?"

Jim nodded. "Of course. Don't be silly. There's no way you could have gotten that disk. You don't have access to the CAD room. Someone had to have taken it from there and planted it in your purse."

Matt took hold of her elbow. "Excuse us," he said, then led her toward the door.

"Hey!"

Matt and Sara turned back.

"What about Friday?"

"We'll talk about that another time," Sara said. "Okay?"

Jim nodded, looking like the poster boy for the National Concerned Society. Matt didn't buy it for one second. He continued taking Sara out of the cafeteria, and once they were alone in the hallway, he stopped. "Do you have any idea who could have put this in your purse?"

She shook her head. "No. I've been in my office all morning. I haven't seen anyone."

"Did you leave your purse alone at any time? To go get coffee, or to the rest room?"

"I did go to the ladies' room, but Juliet was still there. She wouldn't have let anyone touch my purse, or anything else of mine." Her brows furrowed a bit, and Matt was taken aback at the physical effect that little move had on him. He sucked in his breath and held it, focusing on the tilt of her head, the way worry darkened her eyes. He had to force himself to think about the problem at hand.

"Did anyone bump into you on your way to lunch?" he asked, still struggling to focus.

She shook her head. "No. Maybe. I don't know."

He pocketed the disk. "You think about that, okay? Try to recall everything that you've done today. Even something that doesn't seem relevant."

She nodded and looked into his eyes. The trust he saw was slightly unnerving. "Thank you," she whispered.

"For what?"

"Believing in me."

"You're still a suspect, Sara," he said. "I'm sorry, but that's the truth."

"Of course. But thank you anyway."

"Go on back to work. Think about what I said."

She reached over with her hand and touched him on the upper arm. Her fingers were so small, and yet he felt the touch all the way through him. Then she leaned forward, rising on her toes, to kiss his cheek. It was a light kiss. A gentle whisper. But it made him want to take her in his arms, to kiss her the way she needed to be kissed. Instead he nodded, then walked away.

His first stop was the CAD room, where the disk had been stolen. Three people worked in there, and Matt had been studying each of their personnel files. Unfortunately none of them seemed likely candidates.

Lena Khalek had worked for the company since she'd graduated from college two years ago. She was unmarried and made a nice salary. Peter Wellington had a wife and two kids, but he had none of the markings of a company thief. He was too timid to do anything to rock the boat. Terry Southwick wouldn't steal a paper clip from the trash can.

He knocked on the door and Terry let him in. Matthew didn't speak to anyone just yet. First, he walked around, trying to figure out how someone could have gotten out of this room with the disk. The security measures in here were as thorough as they could be, without doing strip searches. No one walked in or out without ID, no one touched anything without direct supervision. Two cameras were set up to sweep the entire area. He'd looked at those tapes over and over, and he'd seen nothing suspicious.

Now he moved over to the far wall where the disks and programs were stored. As he reached for the lock on the cabinet, he sneezed. And kept on sneezing.

Everyone was staring at him, but he couldn't stop. He was racked with sneezing, his eyes watered and he wasn't doing too well on the breathing front. Then he noticed something on the floor near the side of the cabinet. Something white.

He picked it up, still sneezing to beat the band. It was a handkerchief. White. Lacy. Feminine. It smelled like perfume. In a sudden burst of clarity, he realized where he'd smelled the perfume before. On Sara Cabot's neck. Right before the start of his sneezing epidemic. He took another whiff to make sure, and he nearly sneezed his head off.

When he could focus again, he saw the small embroidered initials in the lower right corner of the delicate lace. *SC.*

# *Chapter Eleven*

"Matt's coming over," Sara said into the phone as she tried to put on mascara.

"That's very good."

"But what am I going to do?" She botched her makeup and had to wipe it off and start again.

"I'd say for tonight, use seventeen and six."

"I don't have the book with me, Juliet, and I'm so frazzled I can't think." She put down the mascara, and picked up her blush. But then she didn't have a free hand to use, so she put that back down again, too.

"Wear his favorite color. And ask him the big question. Voilà."

"Oh, no. Not the big question."

"But of course the big question. It's time."

"I don't know what kind of questions he's been asked before, so how can I ask him an 'I've never been asked that question before' question?"

Juliet's laughter didn't help her mood one bit.

"*Chérie,* he's been to your apartment before, and you weren't this nervous."

"That's because he didn't think I was Mata Hari before. He hadn't seen me kiss Jim before. He hadn't developed his allergic reaction to me before."

"None of that will matter tonight. Trust me."

"That's easy for you to say. You're not the one he caught practicing romantic conversations in the ladies' room."

"Don't worry about that. According to his handwriting, he's very kind. But we knew that already, didn't we?"

"Kind is one thing. Falling in love with a crazy lady is another thing altogether.

"Breathe deeply, Sara. Have yourself some wine. Then let nature take its course. You have my word that everything will work out."

Sara looked at herself in the bathroom mirror. She was wearing a ratty pair of shorts and an old T-shirt. Her hair was piled high on her head, held up by an assortment of colorful clips, none of which matched anything she was wearing. She had one eye madeup, the other was bare. All in all, she looked like hell. "Deep breathing," she said. "Right. That's the ticket."

"Save that sassy attitude for him, *chérie.* Now go on. Get dressed. And remember to use safe sex."

Sara blinked. "I'm not going to—"

"That's up to you. But if you should…"

"Good night, Juliet."

"*Bonsoir,* Sara."

She clicked off the phone and got busy applying makeup to the naked eye while she tried to think of what to wear. He liked blue. She had blue clothes. She could do this. Once again, maybe for the tenth time since he'd called, she wondered if he was coming over because he really believed she was the company thief. She'd tried like crazy to figure out when someone could have dropped that disk into her purse, but nothing came to mind. She'd also tried to figure out who would do such an awful thing. She'd never thought of herself as a person with enemies, but there was at least one person walking around who disliked her enough to try to get her in trouble. Big trouble.

MATT WAITED FOR HER to answer the door. He felt nervous, which really ticked him off. Why should he be tense? She was the one with the explaining to do. The disk had been in her purse, the handkerchief had her perfume and her initials on it. He was here on business, pure and simple. Nothing more.

He knocked again, and the door opened. Sara gave him a tentative smile, then stepped back so he could enter.

She was a vision in blue. Her slacks were navy, her blouse pastel, her earrings a combination, and she'd pulled back her hair with a blue headband. It surprised him that he noticed her wardrobe at all.

Normally, unless a woman was wearing something outrageous, or nothing at all, he didn't pay attention to that kind of thing. But she looked really nice. Yeah.

She shut the door behind him. "Can I get you some iced tea?"

He nodded, suddenly very thirsty, and followed her into the kitchen. With her blouse tucked in like that he had an excellent view of her derriere. It was a very nice derriere. A world-class derriere. He studied so hard, he felt sure that he would be able to identify her derriere from every other derriere in the world if he had to. Although he doubted he'd ever have to.

"Sugar?"

She turned around, and he tried to look innocent. "No, thanks."

She poured him his drink, then her own. He found himself looking at her hands. Beautiful hands. Delicate. Soft, with gently curved nails. No polish. Just shiny clean and smooth.

"Is something wrong?"

He looked up at her. She had a little worry line between her brows, a vertical furrow that was as pretty a thing as he'd ever seen. "No," he said, still staring at her forehead. Then he moved down just a fraction and met her gaze straight on. It turned out to be a mistake.

Just looking at her eyes made him want to take her in his arms. He wasn't sure what the connection was, and it didn't matter. The signal was clear, his options narrow. He stepped forward. And made her spill tea all over the floor.

He jerked back to reality, not sure when he'd left, or why. It was like coming out of a dream. For a second he was disoriented, but that passed quickly when he reached for a paper towel. She reached for it at the same second, and their hands touched. Another jolt went through him. Just that little touch had done it. Had made him suck in his breath and hold it, anticipation swirling inside his belly. She let go, and the disappointment was a tangible thing, like a soft blow.

He shook his head to clear his mind of all the foolish thoughts. But he could still feel the echo of her fingers on his.

At least he had the presence of mind to get the damn paper towel and wipe up the floor. That helped. He felt normal again. Well, almost. He was all right as long as he wasn't looking at her.

She'd moved over to the table, and she looked up at him as he came to join her. "You wanted to ask me some questions?"

He nodded, focusing hard on his purpose. "Did you come up with anything? Remember someone bumping into you?"

"No. I tried. Honestly I tried. But I don't remember."

He reached into his back pocket and pulled out a

plastic bag. Inside was her handkerchief. "Recognize this?"

She took the bag from him and studied the white lace. "It's mine. My grandmother gave it to me for my eighteenth birthday. How did you get it?" She started to open the plastic bag.

"No! Don't. It's got your perfume on it, and I'm allergic."

She looked puzzled, and brought the bag to her nose. Opening it just a hair, she sniffed. "Obsession."

"Hmm?"

"The perfume. It's Obsession."

"Do you wear that a lot?"

She shook her head. "I didn't own it until yesterday. Jim gave me a bottle. In your office. Remember?"

Matt sat down. "Well, damn."

"Do you think?"

He shook his head. "Why? It doesn't make sense. He owns too much stock. He's stealing his own money."

"Maybe it's just a coincidence."

Matt studied his hand. "I don't believe in coincidences."

"Maybe someone's trying to set him up."

"By setting you up?"

She nodded. "Why not?"

"Don't you think that's overkill?"

"I have no idea. I've never dealt with anything like this before."

"I have. And this doesn't make sense."

"Why *do* you do this?" she asked. "I mean, why investigation work?"

He took a drink of tea, then looked at her. God, she was so beautiful it hurt. "I got into security while I was in the Navy. It intrigued me. I thought about being a cop, but I wanted more independence."

"Are you happy?"

He wished she would change the subject. "Happy isn't part of the equation."

"Is there something else you'd rather do? A dream, maybe?"

He thought for a long while before he answered. He'd kept the lid on this stuff for a long time, and he wasn't sure it was wise to open up the subject again. Then he looked at her face, and he knew he couldn't lie, or even evade the question. "I did," he said. "I wanted to have my own security firm. I wanted to work with international clients, designing security plans."

"And you don't want that anymore?"

"I'm not sure yet. Marsh has offered me a permanent position. But I also have a job at the Pentagon, if I want it."

"What's the difficulty?" she asked, with the perfect ease of someone who'd never had to make the tough choices. "It sounds to me like something happened before you came here. Right?"

"It was nothing. Nothing dramatic at least. I left the Navy and got offered this job. It seemed like a good choice at the time."

"But you don't want to stay, do you?"

"Maybe."

"That's not the whole story. Come on, look at me."

He did, reluctantly.

"What really happened?"

"There was a woman." He waited for Sara to say something. When she didn't he took another sip of tea, then put down the glass. "We met in high school. Got engaged in college. Then I went into the Navy. While I was gone, she found someone else. It was no big deal."

"Of course it was a big deal. You loved her."

He nodded. "Yes, I did. But that's water under the bridge. I took this job so that I'd have some time to reevaluate my career goals."

"Well?"

"Hmm?"

"What have you discovered? You're a very bright, intuitive man, Matthew. You could have the world on a string. But you have to have dreams."

"No. *You* have to have dreams. I just have to have a job."

"Oh, for heaven's sake. Of course you need

dreams. You have to want something. Something for you. Something that will make you happy."

He met her gaze and didn't move. "There is one thing I want."

She didn't say anything. Her eyes widened and her mouth opened just a little bit as she breathed deeply. Then, she blinked, turned away. "No," she said. "Don't do that. Don't mix the two. If you want sex with me, we can talk about that later. But not now. Now, it's just an excuse to avoid something difficult in your life. I don't want to be an excuse."

"Gee, Sara, maybe you should try saying what's on your mind sometime."

She smiled at him. "I do tend to jump in feet-first."

"We'll come back to certain aspects of your speech later, I promise. But for now, why don't you tell me about your dreams?" Matt needed her to talk for a while. Just to take his mind off the idea of having sex with her, as she'd so delicately put it. It was hard, though. In both the figurative and literal sense.

"I love my job," she said. "More than anything. I can't see changing anything there."

"But?"

"But, I want all the other normal things. A husband, children, a house, a cat and a dog. I'm so-so on the white picket fence, but I do want a garden in the backyard."

He studied her face, her look of innocent expectation. "It's not that easy," he said.

"I know. Believe me. I've had so little experience. Men continue to bewilder me. Every time I think I have them figured out, they go and do something that knocks me for a loop."

"That makes you a member of a very large club."

"It just seems to me that if it's ever going to work between men and women, they have to start telling the truth."

Matt almost said something about the flirting book he'd found in her office. How was setting up a husband-catching battle plan telling the truth? "You mean there should be no duplicity at all?"

"No. Maybe. I don't know. According to Juliet, duplicity in the search for love is not just suggested, it's mandatory."

"Juliet?"

Sara nodded. "And she's been so happily married for so long that it's hard to argue with her."

"Uh-huh. So Juliet thinks you need to manipulate a man to get him to love you?"

She winced. "It sounds a lot better when she says it."

"I'll bet."

"But it should never be hurtful. In the end, all that matters is that both people are happy. That love is equal and respectful."

"Ah, there's the rub."

"Hmm?"

"That equal and respectful part is a doozy. It's a rare thing, Sara. Looking for it, expecting it, can cause a lot of pain."

"So you shouldn't keep looking? Just because you might fail? That makes no sense."

"Why not? It's very practical."

"And it's not living." She got up from her chair at the far end of the table and moved right next to him. She took his hand in hers and looked at him earnestly. Passionately. "I've got a theory about that," she said. "There are only a few things in life that change everything. That turn a person's world upside down. Having a child is one. Losing someone is another. And falling deeply in love is maybe the biggest one of all."

He liked it when she touched him. The feel of her skin. The smallness of her hand. But he paid attention to what she was saying, too.

"If we miss out on even one of those events, we haven't really gone the distance. We haven't tested who we are or what we're made of. Taking the easy way out is a cheat. A big cheat. The stuff worth having are the things that make us lose our sense, abandon old beliefs, throw caution to the wind. Safety is fine when you're around heavy machinery, but when you're talking about your heart, safety is a slow, withering death."

"Wow, that's some theory."

"But don't you think? I mean why would it be

available if we weren't meant to experience it? What would be the point?''

He stopped for a minute. She made sense, in a weird sort of way. ''I don't know what the point is. Maybe it's just to find out what our boundaries are.''

''Exactly. I don't want to look back on my life and regret what I didn't do. That's got to be the worst torment there is.''

''There is an argument for caution, you know. Getting hit by a car would change everything in your life, but you don't want to run out on the freeway.''

She nodded. ''Okay. I'll grant you that. But the other risks, loving someone, giving yourself to that person, are too important to avoid because of fear.''

Matt caught her gaze and saw her fire. It was intoxicating, dangerous. He felt as if he were being drawn in, pulled by a force that brooked no quarter. The crazy thing was, he didn't mind one bit. Not if the reward was Sara. Not if he could have that fire. ''You know what I'm afraid of?'' he whispered. Then he leaned forward.

Sara's eyelids fluttered closed. Her senses became so acute she could smell the soap on Matt's skin. His lips were hungry, and his kiss aroused that same hunger in her. It started low in her stomach and spread out in all directions, settling in her most sensitive regions.

She shifted in her chair, not wanting to move at all for fear he would stop, but the sensations were too strong. It was unlike anything she'd felt before, an urgent, throbbing need to have him touch her.

He took away his kiss, and she moaned. It surprised her, that moan, but then everything about this relationship with Matt surprised her.

His hand came up to her cheeks, and she felt his knuckle gently caress her from her chin to her temple. All the while, his gaze was on her, unwavering and intimate. "I'd better go," he said.

"Why?"

"Because if I don't, I won't stop at kissing you."

"I see."

"Do you?"

She nodded, then brought her hand up to capture his. She held it steady and open and rested against it. It smelled faintly of soap, and more than that, of Matthew himself. She knew she would dream about that smell. "Don't go."

"I have to."

"No, you don't."

He pulled his hand away gently while he broke their eye contact. Sara sighed, and nodded. "Of course you do," she said.

"It's not that I don't want to stay. But it could complicate things. Especially with that whole business at work."

"Ah, work. Yes, I see." She stood up to take her glass into the kitchen. Her disappointment felt like a heavy weight on her heart, making it difficult to move at all.

"No, you don't." He stood up and came after her, but she didn't turn around. She didn't want him to see her face. If he did, he would see that she had no compunction about making love with him. She didn't care about the office thefts, she didn't care that if things went wrong it could be awkward, she didn't care about anything except putting out the fire inside.

"Sara."

She nodded, then turned on the faucet to rinse her glass.

"Turn around."

She stilled, unable to move at all. She felt his hand upon her shoulder. His grip tightened just enough to turn her around. Although she faced him now, she wouldn't look up. She just stared at his necktie.

He touched her with his finger beneath her chin and lifted her head. She tried to close her eyes, but it was no use. Once he'd captured her gaze, she was transfixed. Completely unable to look away from his haunting blue eyes and the meaning she saw within them. He did want her. He wanted her with the same intensity as she wanted him.

"I can't take you to bed," he said. "It wouldn't be right for either of us."

"Don't speak for me, Matthew."

"All right. It wouldn't be right for me."

"Is it because I'm a virgin?"

He blinked. "What? No. Yes. I don't know. That's part of it."

"What's the rest of it? Please tell me. And don't try to blame work."

He sighed, looked up to the ceiling for a second, then met her gaze once more. "I don't want the responsibility," he said. "I know that sounds awful, but I don't mean it that way. You're a very sweet girl, Sara. Sweet and innocent and naive and so beautiful it tears me up inside. I've learned something about you over the last few days. You're a hopeless romantic. For you, it's got to be all or nothing."

"You're wrong," she said. "I'm a *hopeful* romantic. I believe in love. And whether or not you like it, I believe I'm falling in love with you."

He shook his head. "Don't. You'll only be disappointed. I'm not the right man for you, Sara. Not even close."

"May I ask you something?"

He hesitated for a second, then nodded.

"If I wasn't a virgin, would you take me to bed?"

"No, Sara. It's not about that."

"If I promised not to want more, would you take me to bed?"

He shook his head. "You've got this all wrong, kiddo. I'm not worried about you wanting more. I'm worried that I'll want more. That I'll want it all."

"But you can have that."

He brought his finger to her lips. "Hush. Don't

say that. Don't even think that. You haven't lived at all, Sara. You don't know what's out there.''

She took his hand away and glanced around her kitchen. "I know what's in here," she said. Then she moved his hand to her heart. "And what's in here."

He pulled his hand back gently but firmly. "May I ask you something now?"

She nodded.

"How many men have you kissed?"

She didn't have to think long about that. "Two."

"How many men have you dated?"

She looked down at her feet again, absurdly embarrassed. "None."

"How many times have you been in love?"

"Enough," she said. "I get the point."

He took her hand in his and squeezed. "You think you're falling in love because it's all so new. But it won't last. It can't last."

"You don't believe I know my own heart?"

"No. I don't think you do."

She smiled. "You're quite wrong about that, Mr. Quartermain. Quite wrong indeed."

# Chapter Twelve

"Did you sleep with him?"

"Juliet! If I did, I wouldn't say. That's just—"

"The interesting part."

"The *private* part."

Juliet sadly shook her head. "After all I've done for you."

Sara got up from her desk and went to the teapot. She hadn't slept with him last night. In fact, she'd hardly slept at all. "The guilt won't work, Juliet."

"It usually does."

"Not today, okay? I'm tired."

"Ah, so you *did* sleep with him!"

Sara turned to her friend. She was about to admonish her once more, but she realized it would be futile. Juliet would get it out of her, if not by guilt, then by trickery. "It's a good thing I'm not an international spy," she said.

"What?"

"I would break in a heartbeat. They'd just have to look at me sternly and I'd tell everything. I'd probably spill my guts the moment I saw someone from the other side. Especially someone from the French side.''

"We're allies."

"I know. I was being facetious."

"And I was being metaphorical."

"Oh."

"So tell me what's wrong. You don't have to tell the private parts, but I do want to know why you have that sad look on your face."

Sara went back to her desk and dunked her tea ball in and out of the hot water. "I offered," she said. "He turned me down."

"He what?"

"Don't make me repeat it, please."

Now Juliet got up and went to Sara's desk. She pulled a visitor's chair up close, then sat down and leaned forward. "There has to be more than that. *Non?* An explanation?"

Sara sighed, and kept on dunking. "He said I should go out more. Date other people. That I didn't have enough experience to know whether I was in love or not."

Juliet nodded. "Go on."

"That's it."

"No. There's more."

"You mean about the woman who left him?"

"Bongo."

"Bingo."

"Ah, yes. Bingo."

"They were high school sweethearts. She left him when he went into the Navy."

"Ah, so he believes women are fickle. That he can't trust them."

"He can trust me."

"He doesn't know that, *chérie.* You have to help him discover that for himself."

"How?"

"Take him out tonight. Stop by your mother's house. Let him get the feel of the family."

"He'll run."

"No, he won't. He'll learn."

Sara stared at her dark tea wishing she knew how to read the leaves. Even without the fortune-telling, she knew what she was going to do. "All right."

"*Très bon.* Oh, and Sara. Don't forget to practice with the condoms."

"You're incorrigible."

"Yes, I know," she said, smiling. Then Juliet stood up, put the chair back in place and went to her own desk.

"What if he doesn't want to come with me?"

"Of course he does."

"But last night—"

"Trust me. He wants to come."

Sara sipped her too-strong tea. "I don't know why I listen to you."

"Because I'm always right."


MATT LEFT MARSH'S OFFICE, satisfied that his plan was going to work. He just wasn't sure when. He hoped it was soon. He wanted this thing done. Over. Gone. But then he'd have to make a decision about the Washington job. Or staying here.

Staying here was looking better all the time. He didn't kid himself—he knew why. It was Sara. Despite his excellent reasons for staying the hell away from her, he wasn't going to. That didn't mean he was going to fall in love with her. Not a chance. He knew better than that. But he did like her company, and he liked the way he felt around her. As long as he remembered the score, it shouldn't be that difficult. He just had to keep things in perspective.

Besides, she'd really made him think about some important issues in his life. She was right—he didn't have any dreams. He'd put a stop to dreams years ago. So now he had the life he deserved. Isolated. Lonely. Nothing had touched him for a long, long time. And then came Sara. She'd knocked him for a loop. That little innocent young thing had turned his world upside...

He stopped in the middle of the hall. Her words echoed inside him, and he saw her face in his mind's eye as he listened. *"There are only a few things in life that change everything. That turn a person's world upside down. Having a child is one. Losing someone is another. And falling deeply in love is maybe the biggest one of all."*

Matt shook his head trying to clear his mind. It wasn't possible. He *didn't* love her, dammit. Lusted

after her, sure. Who wouldn't? Liked her, of course.
She was a very nice person. But love? No way. Not
him. Uh-uh.

"Matt?"

He heard her voice again, even more clearly. Then
he felt a hand on his shoulder and he spun around
so quickly, Sara gasped in surprise. At least he knew
she was real, and not some nice little voice in his
head.

"You scared me," she said.

"I'm sorry. I didn't hear you coming."

She relaxed once more. He knew her well enough
now to tell when she was tense, when she was calm.
When she was aroused.

"I was wondering if you'd like to come to dinner
tonight?"

No. He shouldn't. She was everything he didn't
want. Ingenuous. Untutored. Willing. He was already in trouble, and going out with her again would
be just plain stupid.

Then she turned her head slightly to the side. Just
a bit. Just enough to loosen one small tendril of hair.
He reached over and touched that tendril, pushed it
back with great care. He marveled again at the feel
of her. The smell of her, all sweet and clean with a
hint of roses. The look of her in her white blouse
and her blue skirt.

"Will you come?" she whispered.

"Of course," he said. He leaned forward to kiss

her, but then he heard a door slam, and he pulled back. Not here. Not now.

She nodded. "Eight o'clock?"

He nodded, too.

She turned to go back to her office, and he stared after her. He kept staring until she'd gone, and long after.

SARA WAS DRESSED IN BLUE again. She'd worn a dress this time, a pastel blue with tiny white flowers. She'd done her makeup and her hair. She'd even changed purses. But even with all that, it was only seven.

She paced back across the living room, but that wasn't getting her anywhere. She needed to do something purposeful. Something that would take her mind off the ticking clock. And she knew just what that would be.

Hurrying now, she went to the kitchen and pulled a banana from the bunch on the counter. Then she went to her bedroom, to her closet, and pulled out the box that she'd put next to her ice skates. With both in hand, she went to the living room and sat on the couch. She opened the box, and stared at the gross of condoms she'd bought just two weeks earlier. She hadn't known what to expect, but it wasn't the small, round, hard circles in front of her. Somehow she'd imagined that they came preshaped. But then men weren't all the same there, were they? She looked at the banana and finally understood her assignment. That Juliet was some piece of work.

With a giggle, Sara opened the first package. The rubber itself felt very smooth, very thin. She remembered to leave a little space on top as she put it on the banana. Unrolling it wasn't as simple as she'd thought, but that was mostly because she couldn't get the banana to stand still. Finally she propped it between her knees and held tight, then used both hands to unroll the prophylactic.

For a moment, she just studied her handiwork. It looked fine to her. Except for that little spot near the bottom. Bringing the banana up close, she saw that the spot was really a tear. She must have torn it when she'd lost her grip. That wouldn't do.

She discarded condom one, and went for condom two. This time, she anchored the banana before she began. Once the rubber was out of the package, she carefully, delicately, put it on the fruit, then rolled it down. Perfect. Except for that little space on top. That was supposed to be important. She took the tip of the rubber and pinched then pulled it up. It worked, but she had the distinct impression that if she'd been experimenting with the real McCoy, that pinch and pull might have raised an objection.

Off with number two, and on to number three. This time she did a fairly decent job. No tears. Roomy on top. A little twisted toward the bottom, though.

She was working on number seven when he

knocked. Sara panicked. There were condoms everywhere. She'd dumped the box on the couch after number four. What would he think? "Just a minute," she yelled.

As quickly as she could, she stuffed the condoms underneath the couch cushions, trying to spread them out so there wouldn't be a lump. Then she stuck the banana behind the big pillow, all the way at the edge of the sofa. After a quick glance to make sure she'd gotten them all, she straightened her dress, put on a smile and went to the door.

MATT WAS SURPRISED at how comfortable he felt with Sara's mother and grandmother. Both women were beautiful in their own way. Her mother, Elaine, was taller than Sara, a little rounder, but they looked very much alike.

Teresa, her grandmother, was elegant and funny. Her hair was completely white, pulled back in a long braid. She didn't look like she was in her sixties, though. There were very few lines on her face, and those that were there didn't take away from her features. She must have broken a lot of hearts in her day.

He felt as if he was getting a preview of what Sara would be like in the future. Time would be good to her.

"Can I get you some more tea?" Elaine asked.

He shook his head. "No, thank you."

"You were telling us about being a SEAL?"

"That's pretty much it. It was good training, and hard work."

"Why did you leave?"

"It was time to go out on my own."

"Good," she said. "My Henry, he didn't like working for anyone else, either. He needed to be his own man."

"What did he do?"

Sara's mother smiled with extraordinary warmth. "He was the best sign painter in the world."

Matt grinned. Her husband had been dead since Sara was a little girl, and Elaine talked about him as if he still shared her bed.

"Momma, don't get started," Sara said. She turned to Matt. They were sitting at opposite sides of the couch, but Sara had her legs curled beneath her. "She'll talk all night about him, if we let her."

"It think that's great," Matt said. "He must have been something."

"He was," Elaine said. "He was kind and good and we all miss him very much."

"I actually liked him better than my daughter," Teresa said with a wink.

"Mom, you stop that." Elaine got up from her wing chair and headed for the kitchen. "Matt, would you like to give me a hand?"

He glanced at Sara and saw that this request hadn't been on the agenda. "Sure." When he stood up, he walked by Sara, and she reached out and gently squeezed his hand for a moment as she smiled up at him. The simple gesture stirred him immensely. He squeezed back, then let her go, even though he didn't want to.

Elaine's kitchen was large and comfortable. He saw where Sara got her taste. The room was filled with knickknacks and mementos, including a picture of Elaine when she was a young woman, with a man Matt assumed was Henry. Even though the picture had faded he could still clearly see the love they had for each other.

His parents hadn't been so lucky. They had fought often, and hard, and finally divorced when he was fifteen.

"Could you reach that cake plate for me?"

He followed Elaine's glance to the top of the fridge. The crystal cake plate was up there with a candelabra, a juicer and a Mr. Coffee. He fetched it for her, then leaned against the counter as he watched her prepare the coconut cake.

"You know, Matt, I met Henry when I was nineteen."

"Oh?"

"He was twenty. He was the first boy I ever went out with. And the last."

"Wow."

"Yes, wow. He was definitely wow. I've never been lonely, either. I've never felt the need to find another man. Do you believe me?"

He looked at her earnest, lovely face. Then her eyes. "Yes," he said. "I do."

"Now why don't you take those plates to the table?"

He obeyed with a smile, never letting on that this little plan had backfired. How stupid did they think he was? He'd already seen how diabolical Sara could be when it came to getting a husband. Now he knew where she got it. They were out to capture him like a fly in a spiderweb. Entice him with cake and tea, stupefy him with soft touches and sly winks. But they'd picked the wrong customer. This boy wasn't falling for any of it. Once he dropped Sara off tonight, that was the end. No more kidding around. She was dead serious, and he had no doubt that her arsenal was full of dirty tricks. Like that little hand squeeze at the couch. She'd known it would get to him. She'd studied his reactions, and figured out that he was a pushover when it came to small gestures. And he'd fallen for it like a big jerk.

"Sit down, Matt." Elaine pointed to the chair at his right. "Sara, you sit next to him."

That proved it. They weren't even being subtle anymore. Grandma was probably going to come right out and ask him if he would marry her little Sara. He knew just how to answer *that* question.

"YOU'RE AWFULLY QUIET," Sara said as they drove toward her apartment. "Is something wrong?"

"Nope. Just tired I guess."

"My mother didn't say something to offend you, did she? Or upset you in some way?"

"No. Really. I'm just tired." He turned at the park, and it suddenly occurred to him that Sirius had probably been trained to perform that trick with the leash and the water. Sara had probably done the training. The dog did seem to like her a little too much. She'd known he would have to take his clothes off. He was just lucky Jim had come over, or else she would have gotten him into bed.

The thought of Jim was equally unsettling. Matt was now certain that he was behind the industrial espionage, and equally certain he wasn't doing it of his free will. It would cost him everything, and one thing he knew about Jim was that he wasn't stupid.

What Matt didn't know was what the pressure was, and who was applying it. But he would, soon enough. He wasn't looking forward to catching him, despite his jealousy over his attentions to Sara. Now that he knew how sneaky Sara really was, he kind of felt sorry for Jim. He'd been put under her spell, too. No red-blooded male could have escaped.

He turned the last corner, then pulled over in front of Sara's duplex. He shut off the ignition, but he didn't take the key out.

Sara looked at him soberly. "Please tell me what's going on," she said. "If I've done something wrong, I'd like to know."

"What makes you say that?"

"I see you don't want to come in."

"I told you—"

"You're tired. Right. It's not even eleven, Matt.

Now come on. Spill. If you don't want to see me anymore, that's fine. I won't like it but I'll accept it. I'm a big girl. I can take it.''

He made the big mistake of looking at her eyes. The hurt there was no parlor trick. It was genuine, all right, and all his fault. "No, I'd like to come in. For a little bit.''

He pocketed his key, then got out to open Sara's door for her. But she was already on the sidewalk by the time he reached her.

"Are you sure?'' she asked.

"Yes, I'm sure.''

She walked him to the door, then led him inside. He actually felt a little better once he'd sat down on her couch. The feel of it was becoming familiar. The light scent of roses comforted him, too. He liked this room. No need to deny it. It didn't mean he wanted to move in here.

"I'll go put up some water,'' she said. "Make yourself at home.''

She left and Matt got more comfortable. He moved a bit. Which made a strange noise. Something he couldn't identify. He moved again. There it was. A squeak? Not really, but he couldn't come up with anything better. Every time he moved, it happened again, so he looked between the cushions to see what was caught. Nothing there. He stood up and lifted the right cushion.

What he saw knocked the wind right out of him. Condoms! Dozens of them! Conveniently located for easy retrieval. My God, it looked like she was ready to take on the Seventh Fleet. And he'd believed her when she'd said she was a virgin. Ha! She was prepared. Ready to rock. Primed to move.

He picked up one packet. It was a good brand, a connoisseur's brand. She knew what she was doing, all right.

He heard her walk out of the kitchen, and he dropped the cushion back down and took his seat. He made his expression bland, bored. Innocent—just like she was innocent.

"If you'd rather have something other than tea, let me know. I still have some wine left. And I picked up some soda."

"Wine?"

"The bottle you brought. Would you like some?"

"Oh, no."

She tilted her head to the side, with a look that was calculated to gain his sympathy, to make him lose his resolve. Not this time. He just looked at her, dared her to try any more of her little tricks.

She looked away, down actually. And her eyes widened with shock. He followed her gaze, and saw that he'd dropped one of her treasures on the floor when he'd lifted the couch cushion.

She looked back at him with a smile that was as phony as a three-dollar bill. He pretended not to notice. Even when she kicked the condom under the couch.

She sat down quickly after that. He could see a

light flush on her cheeks. Her soft, lovely cheeks. She moved closer to him, until he felt her body touch his. His reaction was instantaneous and strong. It was as if someone threw a switch, and his whole body lit up. She must know that she had this effect on him. She'd planned the whole thing. Plotted, schemed...

So why did he want to kiss her? To take her in his arms and hold her? Why in hell did he want to make love to her all night long?

She put her left hand on his thigh. Just a few days ago, he would have thought that was an innocent move. Now he knew better. But knowing better didn't stop the heat inside. It didn't stop him from breathing hard, or from becoming quite physically aroused.

"I should go," he said.

"Okay," she said, moving her hand up his thigh.

"It's late. We have to work tomorrow."

She brought her right hand up, and her finger tickled his ear. "You're right," she whispered.

"We're all wrong for each other," he said, closing his eyes. "You need to get out more. You have a lot to learn."

She leaned over and kissed him on the neck, then nibbled expertly on his earlobe. "Teach me," she whispered.

"Oh, damn." He turned.

## Chapter Thirteen

Sara wanted to think of nothing but his kiss. She wanted to float away with him to that place he'd taken her before. The place where she felt as if the world was filled with magic. Instead she thought about his words of caution.

Was she too inexperienced for him? Should she back off now, while she still could?

He moved his hand down from her shoulder. Softly, slowly, and then his hand was on her breast. All her worried thoughts flew out of her head, and her total concentration focused on his touch.

He circled her nipple with his finger. She moaned, completely transfixed by the sensations in her body. She squeezed her legs together to ease the pressure there, but it didn't help. Despite her innocence, she realized that this new ache could only be healed by one thing.

She reached out tentatively and touched his hardness. The tension in her stomach doubled as she felt him react to her and heard his deep growl.

His hand moved on top of hers, pressing down, letting her know just how much he wanted her. He shifted his kisses to her neck, to the small sensitive area just below her ear.

"What have you done to me?" he whispered, his voice thick and gruff and filled with sex. "Sara. My Sara."

Then he eased her back so she was lying on the couch. He gently maneuvered himself on top of her, although most of his weight was on the couch.

This time, his kiss was urgent. He explored her mouth as if he meant to own it. She felt his fingers at her buttons as he undid each one. When her blouse was open, he slid his fingers across her skin so gently, so teasingly, that she shivered. The feel of his erection on her thigh made her feel giddy with power.

This is what all the fuss was about, she thought. All those poems and songs and love letters. This feeling. It was as if she'd been half-alive. Until he touched her with his hands, with his mouth. With his heart.

When he undid her bra and pulled the silky material away, she felt her nipples tighten. When he touched her with the tip of his finger, she quivered and sighed. When he caressed her with his lips, she cried out.

Nothing had prepared her for these sensations, nothing had prepared her for *him*.

"Matthew," she whispered. "Please..."

"What? What do you want me to do?"

"Take me to bed."

He moved up until he'd captured her gaze. "Are you sure?"

She nodded. "I've never been so sure of anything."

He studied her for a long moment, and for a horrible instant she thought he was going to say no. But then he smiled, and the fire returned to his eyes, and she could breathe once more.

He stood up slowly, careful not to hurt her. Then he held his hand out to her and she rose up and right into his arms. He kissed her briefly, then smiled wickedly.

"What?"

Without a word, he leaned down and lifted the couch cushion. She cringed as she saw the great spread of condoms.

"I wanted to be prepared," she said. "I mean, I thought we might...you might..."

"So all this was for me?"

She nodded.

"I'm really flattered, but I have to tell you I think your expectations are a little bit too high." He reached over and plucked two condoms from the pile. "This is more realistic."

She bent over and took two more. "Let's not risk it."

"What faith you have."

"I've got a lot of making up to do."

His smile broadened. "I guess we'd better get started then."

She smiled back at him. "I think you're right."

Matt swept her up into his arms. He carried her down the hall, into the bedroom, and those last few steps to her bed. She felt like a princess in a fairy tale. When he laid her carefully on her comforter, he kissed her gently on each eyelid, then on the mouth.

She reached up for him, and he sat beside her. It was impossible to move as she watched him unbutton his shirt and take it off. His chest was magnificent. Well muscled, tanned and dusted with dark hair she felt compelled to touch. It was softer than she'd imagined. Such a contrast to the hard muscles below. The maleness of him impressed her deeply. It was so opposite from anything she'd known, yet so right that being with him seemed preordained.

She took off her blouse and tossed it to the floor, but stopped dead still when she saw Matt stand and take off his pants. He stood before her, magnificent. She gasped. "Oh, my heavens."

"I'll take that as a compliment," he said.

"Oh, yes. I never imagined—"

"You keep sweet-talking me like this, and the show's going to be over before it begins."

She didn't want that to happen. Without a moment's pause, she took her bra off. But when he looked at her there, she suddenly felt shy. She covered herself with her hands.

"Sara," he said, his voice so kind, so filled with tenderness she felt silly for her reticence. "I think you're very, very beautiful."

Not quite meeting his gaze, she let her hands go, revealing herself to him completely.

He moaned low and deep. When she did look up, his awed expression made her last vestiges of modesty disappear. Sitting up on her knees, she unzipped her skirt and let it fall. Then it was her panties. After a moment's maneuvering, she was naked, too.

"You're gorgeous," he said, standing still, watching her. Letting his gaze roam freely over every inch of her. She wasn't at all embarrassed by his scrutiny. Not when she could see the want in his eyes.

He climbed on the bed and met her there, on his knees, both of them naked, both locked in a swirl of erotic desire so thick it slowed her movements and made all her senses come alive.

Then it was his chest against hers, the yin and yang of man and woman, the extraordinary way her body cried out for him, and the kisses that were desperate and sweet at the same time.

He took her nipple in his mouth, and she threw her head back and groaned her pleasure. After a long while, when she felt the moisture between her legs, the tightness in her abdomen, and a need so intense it had no words, he laid her down. Only he didn't kiss her, as she'd expected. Instead his mouth journeyed down her body, kissing, licking, teasing her flesh.

When he reached the juncture of her thighs, she thought she would die of pleasure. He was gentle with her, letting her get used to this new sensation. It wasn't long until she started to tremble.

"Come inside me," she said. "Please. I want you so much."

He looked up, then lifted himself above her, hovering for just a second. As he captured her gaze, she felt him slip inside her. She moaned at the unimagined pleasure as he slowly, gently, filled her. There was a moment of stillness followed by a twinge deep inside when he broke her maidenhead. She'd expected it to hurt, but it was nothing.

"Are you okay?" he asked.

She nodded.

His strokes became even and long, filling her, then almost leaving, only to be thrust in deeper. Watching his face, the strain, the tension, the animal force within him, made her want to scream. She felt like an animal herself, a female animal born for this purpose, for this man.

Then, slowly, she began to feel a new sensation. A pulling, tugging desperation that swept away the universe and gave her whole being a single goal. She pushed up to meet his thrusts.

Suddenly he took both her hands in one of his and brought them above her, captured tight at the top of the bed. Without the use of her hands the sensations intensified. There was nothing to do but match his thrusts, hips to hips, thigh to thigh. But it was the look of him, directly above her, held up with his powerful arms, that made her come. She cried out as she trembled violently, as spasm after spasm shot through her body. He pushed into her with all his might, every muscle in his chest and neck as taught as bow strings. His voice meshed with hers in a sound that was sex itself.

Matt let her hands go, and eased himself down until he lay next to her. He'd never experienced anything like this in his life. He'd made love before, but now he realized it had all been a rehearsal for this moment.

He breathed deeply, trying to calm down from the intensity. But he had to look at her. She was so achingly beautiful with her creamy skin, her soft breasts. Her eyes so expressive, he felt for her and with her. Her unabashed sensuality turned him on like nothing had before. The sounds she made were primal and they conveyed everything she needed him to know.

In a flash, the bright flash that comes at that moment of highest tension, he'd known he didn't just want her. He needed her as he needed air to breathe. He would always need her.

He felt her shudder next to him. "Matt?"

"Hmm?"

"Can we do it again?"

SARA HAD NEVER BEEN hungrier. She finished the chicken leg, then began on the salad. Matt, on the other hand, drank a great deal of water, but he just toyed with his food.

"I don't understand," she said. "Is it only women who get so hungry after sex?"

"I don't think it's all women," he said, grinning.

"Oh, so it's just me, huh? Well, it better not happen every time or I'll get as big as a house."

"So you're planning to do this often?"

"Oh, yeah. This beats the heck out of watching TV. I'm surprised people don't do it all day, every day."

"That would be a bit tiring, don't you think?"

She nodded. "There could be rest stops."

He laughed, the sound making her shiver. She marveled at how comfortable she felt, even though they were both still stark naked sitting on her bed. She kept looking at his body. It was so beautiful in every way. So firm, so sculpted.

"Want some more wine?"

She shook her head. "Can you believe we have to go to work tomorrow?"

"Which means I have to go home."

"When?"

"Soon."

"Oh." She'd wanted to sleep with him. To see him next to her when she woke up. Suddenly the pasta salad lost its appeal and she put it down.

"I can't go to work in the same clothes. People would notice."

"You mean Jim would notice."

"Others, too."

"So, you don't want to tell anyone, is that right?"

"I don't think it would be a great idea to shout it from the hilltops."

She stood up and went to her closet. Donning her robe, she turned back to look at him. "Are you ashamed?"

"No! God, what gave you that idea?"

"You just said—"

"What I meant was that we have to be judicious. What would people think if they knew I was sleeping with a suspect?"

"Suspect? You know I didn't do anything."

"*I* know. But, Marsh..."

"He thinks I'm the thief?"

"He hasn't eliminated you as a suspect."

"But didn't you tell him about the Obsession?"

Matt nodded.

She sat down, stunned. "He didn't believe you?"

"He wants proof, Sara. I've got to get him that proof."

"And in the meantime?"

"We have to keep calm. I know Jim is involved, and I've taken steps to catch him."

"I see."

He turned to her and took her hand. "Sara, it's not personal."

"That people I work with think I'm a thief? Call me crazy, but I take that personally."

"It'll be over soon. I swear."

"I'm still having trouble with the idea that Jim is involved. He's your friend."

Matt nodded. "I don't think he's doing it because he wants to."

"You mean he's being forced? Like blackmail?"

"That's my theory, at least. It makes it a little easier."

"But why would he want to implicate me? I've done nothing bad to him."

"You were in the wrong place at the wrong time. I think he's grasping at whatever he can. Which means you'd better watch yourself. Stay away from him, Sara. Things are going to get really uncomfortable for him in the next few days. But then, we'll have him."

"And if he doesn't fall into your trap?"

"I'll think of something else." He caught her gaze and held it steady. "Don't go making more of this than you have to. It's a temporary situation, that's all."

She smiled again, although the tightness in her stomach hadn't left completely. "I do understand," she said. She took his hand in hers. "But I have to admit, it's going to be hard not to shout from the hilltops."

He matched her smile, keeping it just as light and easy. "I know. It was rather spectacular, wasn't it?"

Her shoulders relaxed. "Oh my, yes. And I want to learn more. Lots more. I want to try everything. Well, within limits, but you know what I mean."

She brought her hand to his cheek. "I came to life tonight. The world tilted on its axis. Nothing will ever be the same again."

Matt's smile changed. Not much, but enough to make her notice. The tightness in her tummy cranked up a notch. When he bent to pick up his clothes, she hugged herself. This was worse than the trouble at the office. This was just between her and him.

"Matt?"

"Yeah?" He zipped his pants, then went for his shirt.

"Did I do something wrong?"

He stopped, the shirt on one shoulder. He came to her and kissed her gently on the mouth. "No, darlin'. You did everything just right."

"Really?"

"I swear. You were perfect. Every time."

"It was too much, wasn't it? I shouldn't have pressed my luck."

"I don't think you were the one who got lucky. Of course, I can barely walk now, but that should go away in a few weeks."

"I'm sore, too," she said. "But it's a good sore."

His smile reached his eyes that time, but still, something was off. He kissed her again. She should have felt better, but she didn't. It was only after they'd kissed that final time, at the door, and she'd watched him drive away just as the sun was coming up, that she realized what she'd done. She'd played this all wrong. She'd discarded Juliet's steps. He was scared, and she couldn't blame him. Just because she was certain that he was the right man for her, it didn't mean he'd come to love her yet. Not the forever kind of love, at least.

Tomorrow she would go back to the book. Do just what Juliet said to do. For tonight, well, this morning, she would try to sleep, but her bed seemed the loneliest place in the world.

AT THE END OF THE DAY, Matt left work tired and confused. He'd gotten more information on Jim, but the pieces still weren't falling together. It made him crazy that he was trying to implicate Sara in this mess, and for that, if nothing else, he was determined to put an end to this. He felt sure he could catch him, and prove his guilt, but it wasn't going to be easy. Jim was a clever man. He played his game well, and left few traces. *Tomorrow,* Matt thought. *I'll get him tomorrow.*

For tonight, though, he was going to forget about work, forget about everything. Including, no, especially, Sara Cabot. He'd never felt more conflicted in his life. He was damned attracted to her, there was no use denying that. But if it was only a physical attraction he was dealing with, there wouldn't be a problem. No, this went deeper. She'd gotten under his skin.

He'd considered several options this morning as he drove home from her house—her bed. He'd actually toyed with the idea of going for it. Ignoring his logic altogether. Just loving her.

Then he'd come to his senses. She was Kelly all over again. Only Sara had hooked him more deeply than Kelly ever had. He'd been thrown for a loop, really knocked out by Kelly's betrayal. But it would be nothing compared to the one he was headed for if he let down his guard with Sara.

He'd never felt this way with any woman before. Frankly, he hadn't known it was possible. She was never far from his thoughts. He wanted her all the time, even when she wasn't around. But not just to make love, although that was a very enticing reason. The truth was, he was spellbound. He wanted to know everything about her.

More surprisingly, he wanted her to get to know him. For the very first time in his life, he wanted to share his past, his secrets, his dreams with someone. That scared him most of all. If he told her everything, he'd have no defenses whatsoever. And when she left him, which was inevitable, he had no doubt he'd never recover.

Some tough guy he was. He could stand up to enemy fire, deal with national emergencies, rig explosives like other people set the table. But he was scared of Sara. Scared out of his mind.

He had arrived at his apartment somehow. He didn't remember the drive at all. He'd been on automatic pilot. He parked the car, and when he got out, the muscles in his back and shoulders let him know they were there, and that they needed attention.

Quickly, efficiently, he went upstairs, changed into his sweats and headed for the workout room. A good hour of sweating out the kinks, pushing himself to the limit, was just the ticket. He'd be so tired tonight he would sleep like a baby. He wouldn't think of Sara even once. No sir.

Except it didn't happen that way. He jogged on the treadmill and thought of her at the park. He lifted weights, and she was on the couch. The worst was when he was cooling down. Then, she was in his arms again. Naked. Hungry.

He quit early, and ran upstairs. After a couple of glasses of water and some vitamins, he hit the shower. He didn't even have the guts to make it a cold one.

Twenty minutes later, as he was making his way to the kitchen to fix himself something to eat, the doorbell rang. Maybe it was Sara? The jolt of anticipation took him by surprise. Good Lord, he was well and truly hooked. If he didn't do something about that soon, he'd be a goner.

He opened the door, not knowing whether to hope or worry that it might be Sara. When he saw her smile, he gave up wondering. It was time to worry.

"I took a chance," she said, her smile dwindling. "But you're busy. I'll go."

She turned, but he caught her arm. "Don't be silly. Come on in. I was just surprised, that's all."

She bent and picked up a big paper bag, filled with who knows what, and walked into his apartment. She looked around, and he cursed his decision to hold off on buying furniture. There were two chairs, not very comfortable, and a television set on a card table in the living room. The dining room was almost as bad, what with the condition of the table he'd picked up at a garage sale.

"Your place is... It's very...functional."

He laughed. "That's a nice way to put it. What's in the bag?"

"Dinner. I figured you'd be tired tonight. So I brought a few things. Nothing special, I'm afraid. Just lasagna and a salad."

"Great. I was gonna have a cheese sandwich. This is much better."

She turned to him, and he took the bag from her arms. It was heavier than he'd thought.

"So you don't mind that I've come?"

"No. It's good that you're here. We need to talk. But let's eat first, okay?" He led her into the kitchen. "What do you need?"

"Nothing. Except for you to go relax in the other room."

"No fair. You didn't get any sleep last night, either."

"I took a nap this afternoon. So go."

He snatched a cold beer from the fridge, and then he did as she asked. Once he was in the living room listening to her putter in his kitchen, he realized that letting her in had been a mistake. He thought about her flirting book, which was enough to shake him further. Although part of him was grateful she'd shifted her attention to him, instead of Forester. If she hadn't— Well, he didn't want to think about that. But the other part of him was definitely on guard. She was a wily foe, with female tricks up both sleeves.

No matter what, he was going to end it with her tonight. He wouldn't kiss her or take her to his bed. No way. He was going to tell her it was over. He'd be nice. She'd probably cry. She'd get over it, and so would he. Before any serious damage had been done. Before it was fatal.

After dinner.

## Chapter Fourteen

A delicious smell woke him. He got up quickly, a little disoriented from his impromptu nap. It must have been a long nap, because Sara had set the table, put out candles, even set up a boom box in the corner.

This was dangerous. When he went over to the kitchen to see her, he realized it had gone past dangerous an hour ago. She had taken the safety off, pulled the pin, lit the fuse. Every weapon in her arsenal was right there, in his ill-equipped kitchen.

She'd even worn the jeans he liked so much. The ones that hugged her body and showed off her curves. And that blouse! It was nearly transparent! He could see the shadow of her bra right through it. Well, just in the back, but still.

If he had any brains, he would make a run for it. Just get out. Rejoin the Navy. Go off to the Azores.

"Dinner's ready," she said, with that killer smile of hers. Then she walked over to him, all nice and easy, real casual, and kissed him. Right on the mouth. It wasn't fair. Not when she tasted so sweet, or felt so good in his arms. Who could blame him for kissing her back? He wasn't made of stone, was he?

She stepped back, leaving him primed and ready. Then she got the lasagna out of the microwave. Okay, so she was playing dirty. Two could play that game.

"Matt?"

"Yeah?"

"Do you want to sit down?"

"No!"

Her eyes widened in surprise. "Why not?"

"I—I need another beer."

The surprise turned to suspicion. "I'll bring you one, if you like."

What was wrong with him? Why hadn't he said what he wanted to? Because he was chicken. That's why. Meekly, like the dog he was, he turned and went to his seat. When she handed him his beer, he didn't open it. He didn't deserve a beer.

Sara put the lasagna down next to the salad. She lit the two candles on the table, then went in back of him to light small votives he hadn't noticed before. They lined the windowsill, and when they were lit, they made the room glow softly, especially after she'd turned down the lights.

She was good, all right. Damn good.

One last trip to the kitchen so she could bring out the toasted garlic bread, then she was serving him.

As if he was going to fall for that. Some men would, he knew. Not Mrs. Quartermain's son.

She handed him his plate.

"Thank you," he said, grudging the words.

She smiled as if he had actually been nice. Then she served herself, and sat down in the chair across from him.

He picked up his fork. She did, too. He started eating, determined not to watch her so closely anymore, only he couldn't help it. It was eerie. Every time he took a bite, she took a bite. He wiped his mouth with his napkin, and damned if she didn't, too. He took a drink. This time, she hesitated, but she sipped her water in the end. Something fishy was going on.

He tried one more move—he turned his head to the left. But this time, she didn't mimic him.

Instead she seemed shocked. Her eyes got bigger and bigger, and then she pointed at him.

"What?" he said.

"Oh, no," she said, rising from her chair.

"What is it?"

"Fire."

"Huh?" Then he smelled the smoke. Matt leapt out of his chair to see the curtains behind him smoldering. As he watched, a small yellow flame broke out, and started to spread. He turned to get the fire extinguisher from the kitchen, and then Sara threw her glass of ice water at his crotch.

Sara gasped at what she'd done. He'd moved,

right in her way. Now he was soaked, and the curtain was burning faster.

She ran to the kitchen to fill her glass again, but Matt was quicker. He grabbed the fire extinguisher that hung by the stove. In seconds, even before she'd turned off the tap, he was back out there, and by the time she put down her glass, the fire was out.

"I'm so sorry," she said, desperately wishing she could turn back the clock. "I didn't mean to. I was just trying to make it nice."

He looked at her, and shook his head. He lifted his eyes to the ceiling in exasperation, then turned to her once more. "What am I going to do with you?"

She swallowed. "Forgive me?"

His shoulders drooped. "Of course I forgive you. For the fire, that is. The jury's still out on the water trick."

She was able to smile again. If he still had his sense of humor, all wasn't lost.

"Come on back and finish your dinner," he said, putting the fire extinguisher right next to his chair. "We'll just keep this handy."

"Don't you want to change your pants?"

"No. I think I'll just let them be."

She shrugged and took her chair. "It smells pretty bad in here, huh?"

He nodded. "It'll pass."

She wasn't at all sure why he sounded so resigned. She'd never found him more confusing. No one had to tell her that she'd done step five wrong. It was her first try at mirroring his movements, after all. But he'd been acting strangely since he'd first opened the door. Then she remembered that he wanted to talk, and a cold chill ran down her spine. He was going to tell her it was over. She knew it as clearly and simply as she knew her name. After all this, Flirting 101 had failed. No, that's wrong. *She'd* failed.

There was nothing to do but face the music. She picked up her fork and took a bite of pasta. It was tasteless now, and she couldn't help thinking that it felt very much like the last meal before an execution. He would be killing her, in a way. Killing her heart.

When she glanced up, she caught him staring at her. She tried to smile, but she botched the job. Tears threatened, but she blinked them away.

"Hey," he said.

"Hmm?"

"It's okay."

"What?"

"I don't give a damn about the curtains. I'll replace them. No big deal."

His voice was his voice for the first time that night. The tenderness was back. Dare she hope?

"Let's listen to a little music, shall we?" He said, leaning over to hit the Play button on the boom box. "That should relax us."

The volume was turned up way too high, and the

John Philip Sousa march blared in the room as if the band was marching right there in the kitchen.

He looked at her once more with that bewildered, stunned expression. She couldn't hear him over the music, but she understood his question. He'd mouthed the word, "Sousa?"

All she could do was bury her head in her hands. It *had* been a mistake. She'd snuck out to his car this morning, specifically to find out what kind of music he liked. The only thing she'd been able to see was a Sousa cassette on the back seat. She'd thought it was kind of weird, but then he was ex-Navy. So she'd gotten the same tape. God, she was such a moron! How could she have thought, even for a second—

She looked up when the music stopped. The silence swooped down, wrapping them in awkwardness, filling her with dread.

He took a sip of beer, then put the bottle down. Then he wiped both corners of his mouth with his napkin. He put that down. "At least it wasn't disco," he said.

She laughed. She hadn't intended to laugh. This was serious, darn it. But she couldn't help it. She'd almost burned his house down. Thrown ice water on his crotch. Deafened him with a marching band. And he was glad it wasn't disco.

In a moment, he was laughing, too. For the first time since she'd arrived she felt comfortable. This was her Matt. This wonderful, kind man. Was it any wonder she was in love with him?

"Come on," he said as he got up. "Let's go into the drawing room. Let Jeeves clean up in here."

He held her chair, and when she stood, he was very, very close to her. She looked up at him, a little scared. A lot embarrassed. But then he kissed her, and she knew right then that all was forgiven.

It wasn't a long kiss, but it made up in feeling what it lacked in length. His hug, his touch, his lips all told her she could relax. Except...

She stepped out of his embrace. "You said you wanted to talk."

He paused for a long minute. "It was nothing," he said. "Nothing at all."

"But—"

"It was just about work. About the...Jim situation. It can wait."

The tension in her back eased enormously, but not all the way. Although he'd said the right words, he hadn't looked her in the eye when he said them. Something was still off-kilter, but she wasn't about to press him. Not tonight. Not after what she'd put him through already.

She smiled at him brightly. "Tell you what I'm going to do. I'm going to clean up your kitchen, and then I'm going to go home. Get myself some sleep."

His eyes narrowed. "Are you sure?"

She nodded. "I think it's pretty clear that I'm

overtired. You are, too. I can see that. I shouldn't have come tonight. It was—''

''Nice,'' he said. ''Despite everything, it was really, really nice.''

She put her head down on his shoulder, and rested there for a minute. His hand gently rubbed her back. She could feel him breathe, and soon, they shared that rhythm. It would have been nice to stay that way forever, but she couldn't. She stepped away, out of that safe embrace, and picked up her dishes.

Matt helped her, even though she tried to chase him out. They worked in silence. It wasn't an awkward silence, though. She liked him near her. Liked how he looked with a dish towel in his hand. How his muscles bunched when he reached up to put away the candlesticks. She also liked how his old, worn jeans molded to his butt when he bent down to pick up a napkin. She dropped a fork, on purpose, just to see that again.

But soon it was over. Too soon. Except for the destroyed curtains and the fried paint, the apartment was shipshape once more. All her things were back in the bag. For a moment, she thought of changing her mind. Staying here, after all. Then she caught him yawning.

She went for the bag, but he got there first. ''I'll walk you.''

She nodded.

They walked in silence, too. Easily, comfortably. Every so often they kind of bumped into each other, not hard at all, just enough to touch. Then they were at her car. He put the bag into the trunk and walked her to the door. She turned to say a final good-night, and then she was swept up into his arms and into his kiss and everything was forgotten.

All the passion in the world was in his kiss. The need she'd felt so strongly it made her ache was right there in his lips. He held her so tight, she nearly wept. Not from pain. From gratitude. He did love her. He did.

Then he let her go. And she saw she was right. It was there, in his eyes. But it wasn't the only thing she saw. There was sadness there, too. A deep, hurting sadness that was so intertwined with the love that she could barely tell them apart.

"Good night," he said.

She heard, "Goodbye."

SARA STARED AT THE PAPERS on her desk, but she didn't read the words. Her thoughts were still on last night.

Why did Juliet have to go to the doctor when she had so many questions? Things had shifted last night, but Sara didn't have a handle on exactly how. Was this the normal course of events? When she thought of how he'd looked at her, first with desire, then with that disturbing trepidation, she just got more confused. The only thing she knew she'd done right was leave when she did. It had made for an uncomfortable night. She had slept, but not well.

The whole night, she'd wondered if he was thinking about her. If he was just as unsettled. Or if he had simply gone to bed and slept the night away.

Shaking herself out of her reverie, she closed the report she'd been working on and went to the file cabinet. She bent to put it away, and when she came back up again, she saw a shadow on the wall. At first she thought it was Matt. But something didn't fit. She turned.

It was Jim, standing in her office, smiling at her. It was not a friendly smile, she thought. It was a smile filled with devilment, as her mother used to say.

"Sara," he said, nodding.

"Hi, Jim. What can I do for you?" She kept her voice light and airy, but she sure wished he'd leave. Or that Juliet would come back. That wasn't too likely. She'd left just a half hour ago.

"I thought we could chat," he said, walking toward the door. "I wanted to ask you a favor." He shut the door quietly yet firmly. Then he came toward her again, and it started her pulse speeding.

She tried to tell herself she was crazy. This was Jim, for heaven's sake, not some horrible criminal. Jim wouldn't hurt her. He'd brought her roses, right? But she stepped back when he drew near.

"What's wrong?"

She shook her head. "I think I may be coming down with a cold. I don't want you to get it."

He took one more step toward her. "I'll take my chances."

He stood close enough for her to feel his breath faintly on her face. Jim wasn't as big as Matt, but he was certainly bigger than her. The urge to push him away and run was almost overwhelming.

Then he leaned down to kiss her, and she knew she'd lost her opportunity. She put her hands up between them, and shoved. He missed her mouth when she ducked, but he did kiss her cheek. His hands shot out and he grasped her by the shoulders, pulling her close.

"Stop it, Jim."

"You had *him*. Now it's my turn."

"What are you talking about?" she said, trying not to panic.

"Our bet."

"What bet?"

He laughed, and she felt sick to her stomach. "He didn't tell you, did he?"

She was still pushing at him, trying to get away. "Let me go, please."

He did, holding his hands up in the air and backing up two steps. "Sure. No problem. If he wants more, then I won't muck up the deal."

"Deal? What deal?"

"I know he slept with you the night before last," Jim said, looking wounded, but oddly, frighteningly calm.

"How—"

"How do you think? He told me."

"You're lying."

"Am I? Then how do I know it was your first time? And how do I know that you didn't spend the night last night. But you did have a nice toasty fire, didn't you? Only he doesn't have a fireplace."

She sucked in a breath, and moved away until her back hit the wall. "I think you'd better leave."

"Sure. No problem. But let me give you a little piece of advice," he said. "Matt Quartermain is a specialist in espionage. He'll do whatever it takes to find the company spy."

"Are you trying to tell me that he slept with me because he believes I'm the one?"

"I'm just saying be careful. As a friend. I like Matt, don't get me wrong, but he's pretty determined when it comes to his job. Hell, he even asked me to ask you out, so I could keep an eye on you."

"I don't believe you."

"It's true." He held up three fingers in the Boy Scout salute. "Sweetheart, you and I are at the top of the suspect list. I can prove it."

She started, and he laughed at her reaction. "You think I don't know about the perfume?" Then he got deadly serious. His eyes were what scared her, though. They seemed to belong to a person she didn't know.

"I didn't put that handkerchief in the CAD room. But someone did, just to make me look bad. I'm going to find that someone, and they're not going to like me much when it's over.''

"Please leave," she said. She looked quickly at the phone, but there was no way she was going to get past him to pick it up.

"He wants to solve the case, Sara. Nothing else. You, me, it doesn't matter to him who he brings down. As long as he wins. You got that?''

She could do nothing but nod.

When he smiled again, the light returned to his eyes. How he did it, she didn't know, but it chilled her deeply.

"I like you, sweetheart. I really do.'' He pointed at her with his hand in the shape of a gun. "So you be careful out there, okay? Don't trust so easily. It could be bad for your health.''

"WHAT'S WRONG, *CHÉRIE?*''

Sara didn't know where to start. She was still shaken by Jim's visit, but more than that, she was deeply troubled about her relationship, if she could even call it that anymore, with Matt. When Juliet pulled up her chair, Sara figured she might as well just stick to telling her about Jim.

As she got to the part where Jim tried to kiss her, Sara thought that Juliet didn't believe her. She was having trouble believing it herself. But then she saw her friend's lips come together so tightly they turned white. She saw the flush on her cheeks that signaled her anger. By the time Sara finished, she was far more frightened than she'd been when it happened. Telling it made it more real.

"You think he's right?" she said. "You think Jim was telling me the truth?"

"No, not at all. I think Jim is the one stealing from the company, and he knows Matt will catch him. He's getting desperate."

"Do you think he'll try to hurt Matt?"

Juliet shook her head. "It's clear we don't know him at all. Who can say what a desperate man will do?"

"Then I have to warn Matt."

"Yes, of course. But in a moment. First you tell me the rest."

"What do you mean?"

Juliet didn't even have to say it. She just gave her a look.

Sara couldn't face her. She stared at her hands, instead. "It's over. With Matt, I mean. I blew it."

"Explain, please."

"I just know. It was there. In his eyes."

"Nonsense. You just haven't finished the steps, that's all."

"But I did. Well, almost. I didn't cry fetchingly. I didn't cry at all."

"What did you do?"

Sara swallowed, afraid those tears would come now, even though she'd promised herself she wouldn't. "I cooked his favorite food. I lit candles for atmosphere. I played his favorite music. And I mirrored his moves.''

''But?''

''But the curtains caught fire. The music was all wrong, not his favorite at all. It was Sousa, for goodness' sakes. John Philip Sousa.''

''Go on.''

Sara gathered her courage to finish. ''I mimicked him, but it didn't turn out right. It was like some sort of burlesque. I tried, but instead of making him feel important, I made him question my sanity.''

''But this isn't why you say it's over.''

Sara shook her head. ''You're amazing. How do you know this stuff?''

Juliet swatted away the compliment, then leaned forward. ''Continue.''

''When I got there, he said we needed to have a talk.''

''Ah.''

''Yes, ah. Later on, he said it was about work, but he was holding something back. And then...''

''Yes?''

''Then he kissed me.'' Sara waited for Juliet to prompt her, but her friend was silent. ''A goodbye kiss.''

''He said this to you?''

Sara shook her head. ''He didn't have to. It was in his eyes.''

Juliet leaned back in her chair, and stared at the white wall in back of Sara. Finally, after an interminable wait, she nodded, once. "Okay," she said. "Here's what I think."

Sara was a little afraid to hear. Afraid that Juliet would agree that it really was over.

"I think this is the moment. The moment that will tell."

"Hmm?"

"He didn't say goodbye. He thought he *should* say goodbye."

"I don't see the distinction."

"He's frightened, Sara. Of you. Of your love. But mostly, of *his* love for *you*. It's changed him, and he's not a man who takes to change. He likes his world ordered, and if I know my Sara, you've thrown everything all about. Am I right?"

"Well, only if you count starting fires and dousing him with water. And spaghetti, of course."

"Even more, you've made a mess of his feelings. His safety was in feeling nothing. He can't do that anymore. You made him wake up. Now he's on the brink of sleep again, and it's your job to make sure he gets out of bed."

"Interesting metaphor."

"You understood it, didn't you?"

Sara sighed. "Yes. I did. But I don't know how."

"You do, my darling girl. You do without a lesson. Without a book. Just look in your heart. Tell him what's there. *Show* him what's there."

"And if he still doesn't want it?"

Juliet didn't answer. She didn't need to.

# Chapter Fifteen

Matt leaned forward. He wanted to hear Sara very clearly.

As she finished telling him about her visit from Jim, he had to force himself to sit in his chair and not go right to the bastard's office and break his neck.

One thing was for certain. He wasn't going to wait any longer. He had wanted to avoid a confrontation until he had more direct evidence, but this gave him no choice. He would get the truth out of Forester. Today.

He stared at Sara, looking for any signs of fear or trauma, but she seemed to be okay. It shouldn't surprise him. She was a strong woman. A beautiful woman. No, no time to think about that now.

"How *did* he know?" she asked. "About it being my...first time?"

"It was a logical guess, that's all."

"Why logical?"

How was he supposed to answer that? ''You're very…young.''

''Young.'' She nodded, but he knew she didn't buy it. The truth had seemed indelicate. That with her prim clothes, and her lack of flirting skills up until recently, it wasn't hard to figure out that she was an innocent.

Of course, she wasn't anymore, thanks to him.

When she'd first come to his office looking so grim, he'd thought she was going to tell him she didn't want to see him again. That she never should have slept with him.

It was what he'd been thinking all morning. He'd let his desire for her completely overshadow his own good sense. Even now, as she sat in his wing chair, that desire was there, like a low-grade fever. Dammit. He had to stop thinking about her that way. At least when he was here in the office.

''He mentioned the perfume, huh?''

She nodded. ''He seemed to know all about it. Of course, if he put it there, he would.''

Matt thought about that for a minute. It was a surprise, his coming right out and talking about the perfume. But Jim was turning out to be full of surprises.

''Sara, I don't want you to worry about him anymore. I'll make sure he doesn't bother you again.''

She studied him for a long minute, then said, ''All right.''

He could see she trusted him completely. It was

the same trust she'd given him when they'd made love. The trust of a child who hadn't learned that life wasn't fair. It made him very uncomfortable. Not about Jim, but about the other.

If he'd had any brains at all, he would have left her alone. Not gotten himself, or her, into this mess. It was just plain stupid to be involved with someone as unsophisticated and guileless as Sara. Hadn't he learned his lesson?

Then she smiled at him. It was a gentle, questioning smile. His body, the traitor, reacted to that little grin as if she'd kissed him. That thought just made things worse. Now he was remembering her kisses, and how her naked body felt next to his.

He stood abruptly, scaring her a little. "Thanks for telling me about this," he said, hearing the strain in his voice. "I'll take care of it."

"But..."

He walked around the desk and held his hand out for her. She didn't ask more of her question. She just put her hand in his and stood up.

It was the touch that ruined everything. The way her hand felt in his. It immobilized him, rooted him to the spot. She stepped closer, and then, before he could stop himself, he caught her arms in his hands, and pulled her to him. He kissed her, hard, until he heard her moan.

Not releasing her, he pulled back and studied her eyes, searched for an answer. Why couldn't he say no? Why couldn't he be strong?

"Matthew?" she whispered.

He heard the quiver in her voice. Fear? Probably. "I can't do it," he said. "I tried, but it's no good."

He heard her sharp intake of breath. He saw her flinch as if from a blow. She jerked out of his grasp and ran out the door.

He started after her. She'd misunderstood. But as he reached the hallway, he stopped. Maybe she had read him just right. This was what he'd wanted, wasn't it?

He went back inside. His legs felt heavy, and the room looked dark. Walking to his chair seemed to take forever.

It was the emptiness. The aching chasm in the pit of his stomach. He closed his eyes and moaned. He hadn't known. He hadn't seen it. God, what a fool he was. *It was already too late.* She'd already become a part of him. His heart. His soul. Now all of it was gone. He'd chased her away.

SARA WENT to the ladies' room. She just wasn't up to facing Juliet yet. She wasn't up to much.

She'd been right. He didn't want her. Whatever it was that they had, it wasn't enough for him. *She* wasn't enough.

Why had she ever tried? That stupid book, those silly steps. Nothing good had come from any of it. She'd humiliated herself, and for what? A kick in the teeth? She got some tissue and wiped her eyes, fighting the sobs that were seconds away. She wouldn't cry. She *wouldn't*. Because if she did, she'd never stop.

She checked her makeup in the mirror. It was fine, but it didn't mask the misery etched in her face. So this was love. Well, they could have it. As far as she could see, it brought nothing but pain. Sure there were those glorious moments, making love with him, kissing. But for every ounce of joy there was a gallon of hurt. She'd been so much better off before. When she still had her illusions.

Sniffing one more time, wiping away one last tear, she straightened her shoulder. It would kill her if he realized how devastated she was. She wouldn't give him that, too.

Heading toward her office, her steps faltered before she even turned down her corridor. Juliet would feel so sorry for her. That pity was more than she could stand. It was after twelve. She'd go to the cafeteria and get some coffee. Find an empty table in the back, where no one would bother her.

It was painfully crowded by the time she got there. A long line of chattering employees waited with little red trays. She skipped all that and went right to the coffee urn. Her hand shook as she poured, but she managed not to make too big a mess.

Then she found herself a perfect table. Far away from all of them. Still, she could hear laughter.

She sipped the strong, bitter coffee, then put the cup down. It was time to practice. She pulled the corners of her mouth up in a smile. Even without a mirror, she knew it must look more like a grimace than a grin. So she worked harder. By the time she had to go back to her office, she'd look perfectly normal. If she didn't mess up, she could even fool Juliet.

It took her a long time, but finally she thought she had it. The mask was in place. All she had to do was get through a few more hours. At home, she'd let it go. In the privacy of her bedroom.

What she hadn't counted on was Matthew. As soon as she saw the shadow she knew it was him. Hadn't he done enough to her today?

"Sara?"

The gentle tone almost undid her. A stranger might think that was a voice filled with love. She swallowed hard, forced her smile, then turned to him. "Yes?"

"We need to talk."

"I think we've done enough of that for one day, don't you?"

"No." He went to the next table, took the plastic chair, and put it opposite her. He sat down, and she could feel herself tremble. It would be all right if she just didn't pick up her cup.

"Look, I want to explain."

"I don't need or want that, but thanks for the offer."

"I do. After you left—"

He stopped, and she dared a glance. He looked

so unhappy. She froze as she realized her hand had been reaching out to touch him. To comfort him. Was she crazy?

"I—"

He stopped again, but this time it was because of the PA system clicking on. It wasn't time for Marsh to give his report. Something else must be up.

And then she heard it. Echoing throughout the building, not just the cafeteria. So that every last person who worked here heard it.

Matt's voice. "There's something suspicious about Sara Cabot, that much I know. She was always such a little mousy thing, until now."

A squeal of feedback, then, "You think she's the thief?" It was Jim. Her friend Jim. Jim who brought her roses.

"I don't know. But she is a suspect. So I want you to keep an eye on her."

Everyone was staring at her. Matthew had stood up. His face was so filled with rage she thought he might explode. But it was child's play next to her mortification. She closed her eyes, only it didn't block out the sound of Jim's voice.

"That's not going to be hard. I couldn't help but notice she was damned attractive, even with that royal blush."

"Attractive or not, I want to make sure she's clean," Matt said. "Talk to her. Get her to like you."

"It's a tough job," Jim said, the sarcasm running thick, "but someone's got to do it."

"Never mind," Matt said, loud enough for the world to hear. "I'll do it myself."

Then it was over. The PA clicked off. But now it was worse. Worse because it was silent in this huge room. Everyone stared. Everyone here, in the whole plant, knew what a fool she was. What a stupid, naive fool.

"Sara," Matt said, moving toward her.

She jerked away from him, so hard she knocked the table and spilled her coffee all over. "Don't touch me," she said. Then she stood up, keeping her back straight and her eyes open.

"That jerk. I've got to go after him. Please don't leave. Not before I have a chance to explain."

"I think that was explanation enough." She walked away. The longest walk of her life.

It killed him to watch her. She held herself with so much dignity. Walking past her co-workers, the only thing that hinted that all wasn't well was that she walked a little slow. As if she was finding her footing with each step.

He started after her. He had to explain. She might not forgive him, but he couldn't leave it like this. She'd been battered by him today. He'd come at her with both fists. But she never cried uncle. That just ripped his heart out.

Once he was in the hall, he watched her take those slow, measured steps. His hand went out to her, but he knew instantly that she would never take it. Why should she?

In the hardest moment he'd ever experienced, he turned away from Sara—the woman he loved, the woman he'd shattered. He had to find Jim. Find Jim and make him pay. Not just for stealing the prototypes, but for using Sara so shamefully. For that, he just might get real hurt.

SARA WAS ONLY HALFWAY to her office when Juliet found her. The look on her friend's face, the unblemished pity, completely undid her. She couldn't hold on anymore. The tears came.

Juliet put her arm around her, and walked her to the office. Once inside, the older woman locked the door. Then she helped Sara to a chair.

"I'm so sorry," Juliet said.

"How am I ever going to show my face here again?"

"What? You've done nothing wrong. There's nothing to be ashamed of. You have every right to be upset. To be sad. But ashamed? I won't hear of it."

Sara had to laugh. What else was there to do? "I'll try to do better."

Juliet moaned. "Oh, *ma chérie*. It's all my fault. I'm such a silly, stupid old woman. I should never have gotten you involved in my crazy scheme. I could just shoot myself."

Sara held out her hand, and Juliet took it. "It

wasn't your scheme that was crazy. That was all me.''

"No, no. *Mon petit chou*. Don't you see? It wasn't you at all. Matthew Quartermain just wasn't the man I thought he was. Not by half. I thought he was bright enough to see what a gift you are. That he would welcome you in his heart. But love, it scares him.''

"It scares me, too.''

"Of course it does. For now.''

"Forever.''

Juliet didn't argue, for which Sara was unbelievably grateful. And she got her a whole box of tissues. Sara squeezed her hand again.

"I will tell you something right now,'' Juliet said fiercely. "If Matthew doesn't do something about Jim Forester, I will.''

"What are you going to do? Speak French at him?''

Juliet's eyes narrowed dangerously. "I'll make sure he sings soprano from now on.''

"Now that's something I'd like to see.'' It was odd. She was smiling, and yet she couldn't stop crying. The tears kept flowing hot down her cheeks, and she wondered if they would go on this way forever.

"Are you all right? Can I get you some tea?''

She shook her head. "No. I'm just going to sit here for a while. Then I'm going to take some time off.''

"Hmm," Juliet said, in that tone of voice that meant she didn't approve. "You stay put. I'll be right back."

"Don't leave the door open," Sara said. "Please. Lock it on your way out?"

"Of course, *chérie*." She bent over and kissed Sara on the top of her head, then went to her desk.

Sara just happened to be looking her way when she got the bottle of mace from her purse. "Juliet!"

*"Oui?"*

"You can't use that."

"Why not?"

"Someone could get hurt."

"But of course. Why else would I have it? You're so silly sometimes."

With that, she left, and when Sara heard the lock engage, she thought she was going to fall apart. But she didn't. It was by the skin of her teeth, but she held her ground. Even though those words kept swimming in her head. Matt's words. Matt's true words.

HE MISSED JIM by two minutes at the most. Karen, Marsh's secretary, was badly shaken. "He looked crazy, Matt. Like he was capable of anything."

Matt nodded. "Did he use the stairs, or the elevator?"

"Elevator."

"Did you get what I asked you for?"

She pointed to a file. "It's all there. At first, I thought that's what he was after."

"Thanks. Tell Marsh to get here and stay here. And call the cops. I'll be back."

He took off, toward the stairs. He had the feeling Jim was on his way to his car, and from there? Somewhere far away. Probably out of the country.

Once Matt hit the first floor, he ran full-out. Straight for the parking lot. He almost ran over Juliet. There was no time to apologize, however. He just kept going, praying Jim hadn't made a clean getaway.

By the time he made it outside, he was sure he was too late. But luck was with him. Jim was in his car, still in his parking place.

Matt headed for the BMW. He could see Jim staring at him, then turning to look at the key. But by the time Matt got to him, he hadn't even turned the engine on.

"Get out of there, Jim."

Forester didn't. But he did start the engine.

Matt flung himself at the back door, and it came open at the exact second Jim depressed the automatic door locks. Too late. Matt got Jim in a headlock, and squeezed.

"Unlock the door."

Jim choked, but he found the button and pressed it.

Matt waited for a few seconds, then let go, only

to move as quick as lightning to the front door, which he yanked open.

Jim didn't stir. He just stared straight ahead, the sweat running down his tanned face.

Matt grabbed him by the shirtfront, and forced him out of the car. Forester stumbled, but finally stabilized. Matt wanted to pummel the creep. Beat him within an inch of his life. But he held back. Out of the corner of his eye, he saw that a crowd was gathering near the exit. "Go back inside," he yelled. Then he had no more time for onlookers.

"It wasn't my fault," Jim said, his voice as pathetic as his face.

"Tell it to the cops."

"It was her. She was going to tell. She was blackmailing me. This whole thing was her idea. I swear. It wasn't me, it was—"

"Lilly Marsh."

Jim's eyes widened.

"You think we didn't know? You made phone calls, buddy. Lots of them. To Ralph Marsh, only he was never home when you called. And we logged every one."

Jim came to life. He jerked backward, swinging his elbow into Matt's gut. Matt bent over for just a second, and came up swinging. His fist connected with Forester's jaw, the blow knocking him back against the car.

Matt could see he was dazed, but he wasn't down. He fisted his hands, and went after Jim one more time. But the weasel was fast. He ducked and ran to his right. Just as Matt turned to pursue, he heard Jim scream.

Then he saw Juliet.

And the bottle of mace in her hand.

Forester hit his knees. He continued to bellow, and wipe at his eyes. He'd be out of commission for some time. At least until the cops arrived.

Matt turned to Juliet. "Thank you."

"I should give you a taste of this, too."

"Yeah. I know."

"What are you going to do about it?"

Matt walked over to where Jim crouched and hooked his collar, forcing the crying man to his feet. He heard sirens. But he didn't take his eyes off Juliet. "She won't talk to me."

"And why should she?"

"I need to explain."

"Explain why you've left her?"

"No! Why I need her back."

Juliet, tight-lipped and narrow-eyed, nodded once. "You'll do just as I say."

"What?"

"I brought her to you, you foolish man. And if you want her back, you'll do everything I tell you to do."

The police car pulled up next to him, and Matt let Jim's collar go. "Okay," he said to Juliet. "Anything you say."

# Chapter Sixteen

Sara only took one day off. She'd thought she might stay home for a month, but she was so depressed, and everything in her apartment made her remember Matt, that she gave up and came back early.

It was hard to walk inside. To know that people would stare at her, that they'd gossiped about her and knew her private business. For a few moments last night, she'd considered quitting, but then she'd have to live with being a coward.

Summoning all her courage, she pushed the door open and entered Willard and Marsh. The coast was clear so far and she made her way toward her office, walking as quickly as she could without actually running.

She made it free and clear, backing into her office so she could check the hall both ways. Then she shut the door and sagged against it with relief. She was here, working, but she didn't have to face anyone. Especially…him.

She turned and jumped back in shock, her startled cry loud in the small room.

Flowers. They were everywhere. Roses. Orchids. Lilies. Mums. Every color of the rainbow. In vases, baskets, wreaths and rose petals scattered on the floor and on her desk.

Sara blinked and stared. Then blinked again.

"Good morning, *chérie*."

She jumped again, this time turning toward Juliet's desk, but she didn't see Juliet. A vase moved to the right, and then she saw her. Behind a forest of flowers.

"What's going on?"

"I don't know. But it's pretty in here, *non?*"

"No. It's him. He thinks he can buy me off with petals? No way." She transported the vases and baskets on her desk, putting them on the floor, since there was no place left on the countertops or file cabinets. Then she swept the rose petals off with her sleeve.

Turning to Juliet, she crossed her arms and dared her to say anything in his favor. Her look worked, because Juliet simply shrugged and went back to her computer.

Sara was going to do the same. Just because it smelled intoxicatingly beautiful was no reason to be sidetracked. It must have cost him an arm and a leg, that's for sure. But she didn't care. His attempt at an apology insulted her. As if he could wipe away the hurt by offering her a token. Buy her off so he didn't have to feel guilty. Well, he *should* feel guilty. Feel it till it choked him.

She sat, put her purse in the drawer, flipped on her computer and got busy. She didn't glance to her right or left. Just straight ahead.

Nothing happened again until ten-thirty. That's when the Federal Express man arrived. He put a box down on a bare patch of floor, and as was her habit, she took a moment to admire his rear. But...it wasn't his. This was an impostor. Of course, she knew who this behind belonged to. She could have picked it out of a lineup.

"What are you doing here?"

Matt stood up and turned around. "Can we talk?"

"No."

"But—"

"No." She went back to work, ignoring him with all her energy.

"Okay," he said. "But I'm not giving up."

She didn't answer him.

He walked by her desk, really slowly. Just as he reached the edge, he tripped, and something spilled with a terrible clatter.

She jumped back, gasping, and then she saw what he'd dropped. Forks. Maybe fifty of them.

"It was supposed to be spaghetti," he said.

She looked from his hopeful smile to Juliet, who'd ducked behind some gardenias. She'd deal with her later. For now, it was enough to stop this nonsense. "I don't consider this amusing," she said.

"What you said, you can't take back. I don't want you to. You told the truth, and I heard you. I'm sure we'll be friends again, but not for a little while, okay? The best thing you can do is leave me alone."

The look he gave her tugged at something deep inside her, underneath the hurt. It was a "please" and a "sorry" wrapped into one. Even the remarkable blue of his eyes seemed muted, as if they had no right to shine.

She took a deep breath, and turned away. Eventually she heard him leave. When she could focus again, she realized her hands had been on the wrong keys as she typed, and gibberish covered her screen. At least that was a mistake that could be fixed.

AT NOON, Sara got her peanut butter and jelly sandwich from her purse. It didn't appeal to her, but she doubted anything would.

"What are you doing?" Juliet asked.

"Having lunch."

"You can't eat in here."

"Why not?"

"Because. They expect you to."

"Who?"

"Everyone. They expect you to hide in here like a little shaking bunny. You can't."

"Sure I can."

Juliet walked from behind the curtain of flowers. "No. I won't let you."

"This has something to do with him, doesn't it. You're in cahoots with Matt."

"Cahoots? What kind of a word is cahoots?"

"That's not the issue."

"Of course it's not. The issue is that you have to show these people what you're made of. That you're strong, and proud, and no silly tape is going to make you cower in the corner."

"I can't. I mean it. Not today. Tomorrow I'll face the dragon, all right? Today, cowering makes a lot of sense."

Juliet walked behind Sara's desk. She took Sara's purse out of the drawer, then she grabbed Sara herself by the arm. "Come on. The longer you wait, the harder it will get."

Sara groaned, but gave in. She'd hear about it all day if she didn't. So she'd be humiliated. What's new?

When they got to the cafeteria, Sara balked. She could already see the place was packed. They were all probably waiting for an encore.

Juliet was on to her, though. Sara felt her friend's hands on her back as Juliet shoved her inside the lunchroom.

To her horror, everyone *did* stop what they were doing. They turned, as if they'd been cued, to stare at her. The silence was deafening, and the heat rose in her cheeks until she felt on fire.

Juliet pushed again, a little more gently this time, but Sara got the point. She calmly walked over to the stack of trays and picked one up. She moved to the back of the line, but then everyone ahead of her cleared out of her way. It wasn't just her cheeks on fire anymore. It was her whole face. She even felt her neck redden.

But she went on. She walked up to the salads, and picked up a square of Jell-O mold. Not that she was going to eat it. But it was easy to carry, and Jell-O shook no matter what, right? Her shakes wouldn't be obvious at all.

It got worse, then. As she headed toward a back table, one in the corner, the crowd—and it was one heck of a crowd—actually parted. Like the Red Sea. They left a narrow path for her, right down the middle of the room. The deeper she walked, the more people stood aside, until finally, just before she reached the end of the room, she saw it.

Matt waited for her at a table. Not just a table. A table out of a storybook.

There was a pink tablecloth. Two delicate pink roses in a bud vase. Candles, long and tapered, in alabaster holders. She could see plates and silver setups. Champagne cooling in a silver ice bucket. Then there was the man standing just to the right of the table, the man with the sappy grin and the violin at his neck.

None of it surprised her more than Matt himself, though. He was wearing his worn jeans, the ones she liked so much, topped with a faded red T-shirt that fit him quite snugly. She could see the ripples of his muscles underneath the material, and of course, on his bare arms.

He held a seat for her, and encouraged her to come forward with a nod.

It was crazy. She should run away, run from him. He was dangerous. More so now that he knew how much he could hurt her. But when she turned around, her co-workers had filled in the gap behind her, blocking her escape route.

"Go on, honey," a woman said from somewhere in the crowd.

"Do it, Sara."

"We're rooting for you, girl."

It wasn't fair. None of them knew how he'd broken her heart. How he'd shattered her to pieces. Now this.

She got it, of course. Juliet had given him the book. The forks on her desk was step one. She would bet that the food he'd brought was coq au vin, with chocolate éclairs for dessert. Those were her favorites, and that was step eight. The color scheme—step seventeen.

She turned back to Matt, just to make sure she was right. Then she'd leave, no matter who was standing in her way.

He pulled the chair out further. "For you, Sara," he said.

The violinist began to play. She didn't recognize the tune for a few bars, then she got it. "Nessun Dorma." Her favorite.

Despite her best intentions, her promise to herself, she felt tears come to her eyes. She tried hard to hold them back, but one escaped. She wiped it quickly, trying to get rid of the evidence. She didn't want to let him know that hope had come back. Hope was the enemy. Hope made her dream.

She took another step. Yes, she was right. It was her favorite meal, still steaming. Surprisingly, as she got closer still, she could see the chicken was a little burnt. And the sauce looked a bit lumpy.

Then she was next to him. He smiled at her hopefully, and she wanted him so much it scared her. But before she could run, he touched her on the arm. The upper arm. And he gazed into her eyes.

It was sit down, or fall down. She sat.

He moved around to his seat, while the violin music soared around them. But before he sat, he looked at their audience. "Go on," he said, as if talking to reluctant children. "You're done."

Slowly, hesitantly, she began to see movement. The people on the outer ridges cleared out, followed by the next layer and the next. Oh, they didn't leave the cafeteria. But at least they sat down in a pretense of minding their own business. Some even started talking.

Matt seemed satisfied. He sat, turning all his attention to her. "It's coq au vin," he said, pointing to her plate. "Salad with those little croutons you like so much, and vinaigrette dressing you shake up in the cruet."

She looked at her food, more carefully this time. When she looked back at him, it was with total surprise. "You made this. You made all of this."

He nodded. "For you." Then he reached his hand to her.

She didn't want to take it. If she did, he would win. She'd have let his little flirting gestures sweep away what he'd said. What he'd done.

As if reading her thoughts, he withdrew his hand. He turned to the violinist, and said, "Thank you, Del. Why don't you go around and take requests for the rest of the hour?"

She kept her gaze on Del until she had to face her own music.

"Will you let me explain?" he asked. "You don't have to believe me. You can tell me to go to hell, and I will. I was there last night, so I know the way. But let me try, okay?"

"All right," she said, and the hope she'd been pushing down sprang up inside her, filling her with an anticipation that made it hard to breathe. She bit her lip to keep herself steady. She wouldn't show it. Not yet.

"I kept thinking I was safe," he said. "I figured we'd only known each other a little while. That it couldn't be serious yet. But I knew if I went any further, it would be serious. That I'd fall so deeply in love with you that there'd be no way out. I would need you like—I don't know. Oxygen. And then, when we were through, when you got too curious about what you'd missed, I'd never make it.''

She started to speak, but he put his hand up. ''Not yet. Not till I'm through, okay?'' He took a sip of wine, although he didn't stop looking at her for a second. ''So, even though I wanted you all the time, I figured it would be better for both of us if I said goodbye. Only, I couldn't do it. I tried, but it was no good. It was too late. I already loved you too much.''

Sara felt her heart thrum in her chest. ''That's what you said to me.''

He nodded.

''I thought...''

''I didn't understand at first, either. It was only when you'd left, when I knew I'd chased you away, that I got it.'' He held out his hand once more.

This time, she took it in hers.

''I came looking for you then. I found you, here. I was trying to tell you—''

''When the PA went on.''

''I didn't know he'd taped us,'' Matt said, ''but more than that, what he played back isn't what happened. I do admit that I suspected you. But that was before I knew you.''

''Did you tell Jim to go out with me?''

He nodded. ''It was wrong, and I apologize for that. I corrected that error as well as I could, once I thought about it. But I won't weasel out of it. I said those things. I even went to the park that day, just to try to figure you out."

"But you kissed me."

"That had nothing to do with work. I think it happened when I saw you with that crazy humongous dog. The way you held on to him, even though you knew he outweighed you, he could outrun you. Hell, he could have had you for lunch." Matt smiled. "But you hung on. You didn't care about the odds. You just kept on going."

"I see," she said, amazed the words came out at all. Her head was spinning, and her heart was thumping and she wanted to jump up and kiss him and tell him everything was okay now. Yet she held back.

He moved closer to her. "I've made some decisions," he said.

"Oh?"

"I'm going to stay here, but not at Willard and Marsh. At least not full-time. I'm going to start my own firm."

"My goodness."

He nodded. "I've found my dreams again, Sara. Because of you."

She looked away for a moment, just to get up her courage, then she turned to him. "So what do you want?"

He looked at her with eyes so filled with love that she had her answer before he spoke. "You. Always, you. Forever, you."

Then he was the one who stood up. He was the one who took her shoulders and helped her to her feet. He was the one to kiss her.

Someone started clapping, then the room was filled with wild applause. They parted long enough to smile like kids. Long enough for her to see Juliet, standing just a foot away, tears streaming down her face.

Sara nudged Matt, and he turned, too. Together, they walked to their friend. Matt kissed her on one cheek, Sara on the other.

"We'd like you to be at our wedding," Matt said. "Matron of honor."

Juliet hugged them both. "Thank you, my darlings. But I've already watched your first steps down the aisle. All thirty of them."

When Matt kissed Sara this time, she sent up a silent prayer of thanks. Like her mother before her, she'd met the one man she would love her whole life.

And he loved her right back.

**Head Down Under for twelve tales of heated romance in beautiful and untamed Australia!**

**Here's a sneak preview of the first novel in THE AUSTRALIANS**

*Outback Heat* by Emma Darcy
available July 1998

'HAVE I DONE something wrong?' Angie persisted, wishing Taylor would emit a sense of camaraderie instead of holding an impenetrable reserve.

'Not at all,' he assured her. 'I would say a lot of things right. You seem to be fitting into our little Outback community very well. I've heard only good things about you.'

'They're nice people,' she said sincerely. Only the Maguire family kept her shut out of their hearts.

'Yes,' he agreed. 'Though I appreciate it's taken considerable effort from you. It is a world away from what you're used to.'

The control Angie had been exerting over her feelings snapped. He wasn't as blatant as his aunt in his prejudice against her but she'd felt it coming through every word he'd spoken and she didn't deserve any of it.

'Don't judge me by your wife!'

His jaw jerked. A flicker of some dark emotion destroyed the steady power of his probing gaze.

'No two people are the same. If you don't know that, you're a man of very limited vision. So I come from the city as your wife did! That doesn't stop me from being an individual in my own right.'

She straightened up, proudly defiant, furiously angry with the situation. 'I'm *me*. Angie Cordell. And it's time you took the blinkers off your eyes, Taylor Maguire.'

Then she whirled away from him, too agitated by the explosive expulsion of her emotion to keep facing him.

The storm outside hadn't yet eased. There was nowhere to go. She stopped at the window, staring blindly at the torrential rain. The thundering on the roof was almost deafening but it wasn't as loud as the silence behind her.

'You want me to go, don't you? You've given me a month's respite and now you want me to leave and channel my energies somewhere else.'

'I didn't say that, Angie.'

'You were working your way around it.' Bitterness at his tactics spewed the suspicion. 'Do you have your first choice of governess waiting in the wings?'

'No. I said I'd give you a chance.'

'Have you?' She swung around to face him. 'Have you really, Taylor?'

He hadn't moved. He didn't move now except to make a gesture of appeasement. 'Angie, I was merely trying to ascertain how you felt.'

'Then let me tell you your cynicism was shining through every word.'

He frowned, shook his head. 'I didn't mean to hurt you.' The blue eyes fastened on hers with devastating sincerity. 'I truly did not come in here to take you down or suggest you leave.'

Her heart jiggled painfully. He might be speaking the truth but the judgements were still there, the judgements that ruled his attitude towards her, that kept her shut out of his life, denied any real sharing with him, denied his confidence and trust. She didn't know why it meant so much to her but it did. It did. And the need to fight for justice from him was as much a raging torrent inside her as the rain outside.

# *Presents Extravaganza*

## 25 YEARS!

### It's our birthday
### and we're celebrating....

Twenty-five years of romance fiction
featuring men of the world and captivating women—
Seduction and passion guaranteed!

Not only are we promising you three months of terrific
books, authors and romance, but as an added **bonus**
with the retail purchase of two Presents® titles,
you can receive a special one-of-a-kind keepsake.
It's our gift to you!

Look in the back pages of any Harlequin Presents® title,
from May to July 1998, for more details.

Available wherever Harlequin books are sold.

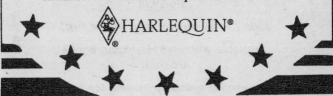

HARLEQUIN®

# MEN at WORK

## All work and no play? Not these men!

**April 1998**

### *KNIGHT SPARKS* by Mary Lynn Baxter

Sexy lawman Rance Knight made a career of arresting the bad guys. Somehow, though, he thought policewoman Carly Mitchum was framed. Once they'd uncovered the truth, could Rance let Carly go...or would he make a citizen's arrest?

**May 1998**

### *HOODWINKED* by Diana Palmer

CEO Jake Edwards donned coveralls and went undercover as a mechanic to find the saboteur in his company. Nothing— or no one—would distract him, not even beautiful secretary Maureen Harris. Jake had to catch the thief—*and* the woman who'd stolen his heart!

**June 1998**

### *DEFYING GRAVITY* by Rachel Lee

Tim O'Shaughnessy and his business partner, Liz Pennington, had always been close—but never *this* close. As the danger of their assignment escalated, so did their passion. When the job was over, could they ever go back to business as usual?

## MEN AT WORK™

Available at your favorite retail outlet!

 HARLEQUIN®  Silhouette®

From the high seas to the
Scottish Highlands,
when a man of action
meets a woman of spirit
a battle of wills—
and love—ensues!

*Ransomed Brides*

This June, bestselling authors Patricia Potter and
Ruth Langan will captivate your imagination with this
swashbuckling collection. Find out how two men of action
are ultimately tamed by two feisty women who prove
to be *more* than their match in love and war!

# SAMARA by Patricia Potter

# HIGHLAND BARBARIAN
# by Ruth Langan

Available wherever Harlequin and Silhouette
books are sold.

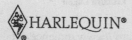 

HARLEQUIN®

A M E R I C A N ◆ R O M A N C E®
®

# COMING NEXT MONTH

**#733  AKA: MARRIAGE  by Jule McBride**
*Big Apple Babies*
When Shane Holiday offered marriage to Lillian Smith so she could adopt a
baby, he did it to get close to the woman he'd tracked for seven years. But
what started as marriage with an agenda suddenly had Shane thinking he
was a husband and daddy for real!

**#734  THE COWBOY & THE SHOTGUN BRIDE  by Jacqueline Diamond**
*The Brides of Grazer's Corners*
One minute Kate Bingham was about to say "I do," the next she was swept
off her feet by sexy fugitive Mitch Connery. Although Mitch was innocent,
Kate's newly awakened desires were not!

**#735 MY DADDY THE DUKE  by Judy Christenberry**
When her grandmother, the Dowager Duchess, put out an APB on her dad as
the World's Most Eligible Bachelor traveling in the U.S. to find a wife, little
Penelope Morris went along with her father's disguise as typical Americans.
As long as he stayed close to Sydney Thomas, who Pen handpicked to be her
new mommy!

**#736  DADDY 101  by Jo Leigh**
Along with the fortune he had inherited, Alex Bradlee got a set of rules for
love. They'd served him well...until he met Dr. Dani Jacobson, who had some
rules of her own, the first of which was "Run—don't walk—away." But her
daughter had other ideas....

## AVAILABLE THIS MONTH:

Look us up on-line at: http://www.romance.net